Volume Three

Airship 27 Productions

TM

The Moon Man Volume 3

Editor: Ron Fortier
Associate Editor: Jonathan Sweet
Production Designer Rob Davis
Promotion and marketing by Michael Vance

Published by
Airship 27 Productions
www.airship27.com
www.airship27hangar.com

ISBN: 978-1-953589-88-0

Printed in the United States of America

10 9 8 7 6 5 4 3 2 1

the MOON MAN
VOLUME THREE

TREASURE OF THE SNAKE PIRATE

by David Noe

"The first thing they want to do is shoot me in the head, and that's a very good thing."

"Still, the thought of you gliding into the middle of a gunfight is a very chilling idea."

"That's the general idea, Ned."

"Is it also the idea to end up dead in the middle of a cemetery?"

"We all end up dead in a cemetery eventually," Stephen pulled the penlight out of his mouth and clicked it off, "At least I'll be in good company." He folded the map and placed it in his breast pocket.

"I don't see how mobsters and corpses are good company," Ned Dargan pulled his driving cap down over his cauliflower ear and squinted from out the driver's side front window, "There's no moon out tonight, Boss. How you gonna see them?"

Stephen Thatcher sat in the backseat of his luxury car and pulled his black slick gloves up over his strong hands. He flexed his fingers and sighed, performance jitters. He still got them sometimes, not as often as he used to, but on nights like this when the moon was gone and the shadows were deep, he could still feel the butterflies in his gut. "The moon's not gone," he reached over beside him to the metal reflective fishbowl helmet in the seat. He put it on over his head and clicked it into place. The penlight hung from a line around his neck and pointed up. When he turned it on, his helmet illuminated like the moon in the night sky.

"I am the moon," he said in a deep voice.

"You are the target," Ned mocked.

"You loaded and ready?" Stephen opened the door a crack.

Ned patted the handgun under his jacket.

"Well, then, we'll both be in good company," Moon Man held up his .45 automatic, "But if you and Sue and my best .45 will be backing me up, I'll be in the best company yet."

Ned rolled his eyes, "We're not taking down a corrupt businessman or cracking a safety deposit box. These aren't white collar crooks. These aren't Dinjab princesses who are throwing a ball in the city tonight, and who we should be robbing instead."

"Yes, I know."

"These are killers and thugs," Ned said.

"I know."

"Guys that'd shoot their own mothers for the fun of it, you know?"

...

"You know, Boss?"

...

"Boss?"

...

"He could have at least closed the door." Ned got out and latched the back door with as little sound as possible.

They were up on a hill overlooking Transport Cemetery, one of the oldest cemeteries in Great City. Occasional gunshots could be heard amongst the tombstones below. At least they had some sort of a plan. Both Stephen and Ned felt a lot better when they actually had a plan. This was a new trick, though. Stephen ran full out at the top of the hill above the cemetery and leapt out into the darkness of the night, head alight and beaming, attracting all the attention. Bullets chased the air around his head and several ricocheted into the night. One of the crooks below was either a very good or a very bad shot. A slug struck Moon Man in the chest, just above the heart.

"Huuckkk!" Moon Man landed and rolled. The flashlight flickered and broke.

"I think we got him!" one of the men yelled out.

"It'll take more than bullets to stop the moon!" Moon Man yelled through his pain.

Shots fired atop the hill as Ned was in place. He let go a volley of blasts and then fired off a shotgun that he'd pulled out from under the seat.

"Who's there?" someone shouted.

"Not another gang!"

"Holy crud! We got us a war zone, here!"

FLASH!

Amidst the scattered gun muzzle blasts, a brighter light popped for just a moment. Moon Man ducked down below the headstones and made his way to the outside of the chaos. There, in the dark, a figure dropped the dimming remains of a camera bulb. Moon Man knew who it was right away.

"Stuart Lee!" Moon Man leapt over to the shadowy figure. "You taking up photography now, Stuart?"

"Jeepers!" the man jerked back from the large tombstone he was in front of, "It's the Moon Man!"

"Beaten up any helpless old ladies recently, Stuart?"

"Go suck an egg, Moon Man!" Stuart cackled, "There ain't nothin' for you to rob here."

"You got an awful smart mouth for someone so stupid," Moon Man swooped up and grabbed him by the lapels, "What's the morning edition?"

"Moon Man robs another gas station, I reckon," Stuart squirmed.

Moon Man swung his arm back in an open handed blow toward's Stuart's face. The punk flew backwards onto the ground and dropped his camera.

"When I ask you a question, Stuart, I expect a…"

Lights and a siren blared up over the hill and onto the grounds of the large estate. The gunfire immediately stopped.

"Jeeze!"

"Move it out!"

"It's the cops!" Stuart got up, holding his mouth, "We gotta scram! Go GO!"

"Run like the vermin in the light!" Moon Man raised his fist and shouted as the police car drove right up to him and screeched to a stop, "Tell Marcetti to watch his back. I know he's listening!"

"Get in quick!" Sue McEwen shouted across the car through an open window, "If Daddy finds bullet holes in his squad car one more time…"

Moon Man picked up the camera and jumped into the squad car. "We have to check on Angel," he said, "He's atop the hill…"

"Flashing his lights," Sue said, "That the signal?"

"He's fine," Moon Man breathed heavily, "Head back to the shop."

"Are you okay, Stephen?" Sue's big dark eyes filled with concern, "You take a slug?"

"I took a bad idea," Moon Man wrestled with his vest and pulled out a bullet slug, "I thought it smart to use this supposed bullet proof vest, but it hinders my movement and feels like I went a few rounds with Joe Louis and he was sporting a baseball bat."

"Was it worth it?"

"We got there before the police did, didn't we?" Stephen clicked his helmet to the side and pulled it over his head, "We'll get this film developed and see what the bait looks like."

The teapot screamed, and the part time crook, Stuart Lee just about knocked over his kitchen table as he jumped up in alarm.

"Shut it! Shut it!" he took hold of the metal pot on the gas stove with his bare hand, "Yeowch!"

He pulled back and wrapped his hand in his worn wife-beater undershirt. He pushed the pot off the flame, and only then got the bright idea to turn off the stovetop.

"It's just the teapot," he said to the silent record player sitting in the corner. The player was new, but it wasn't a player.

He creaked open the cracked yellowed bedroom door and looked in at the darkness. He sighed and latched the door shut again. Two cups now lay on the floor. The one that once held sugar now set overturned on a pile of the sugar it once held. It was cracked, but then most of the things in Stuart's life were cracked. That's why he put sugar in it. Maybe sometimes a little sweet can come out of something that's broken. In this case, the sugar was lost, but it cushioned the cup and kept it from shattering. The empty smaller cup suffered the loss of its handle. Stuart set the cups back on the table. He scooped the sugar up with his hands and put it back in the cracked cup. It seemed to him that he wasn't much good at protecting the smaller cup. He needed to find the handle and glue it back on. That would make things a little better at least, but the handle had bounced off into the dark beneath the ice box. He was squatting down, reaching around the old appliance when the Moon spoke to him.

"Stuart Lee, we need to talk!"

Thunk!

"Ah!" Stuart rolled on the floor, holding his head from the smack on the counter, "Jeez, it's the… Hold on a minute."

He grabbed up the broken handle with his free hand and winced in pain, "Holy smokes, man. Give a guy some warning, would yah?" He stood and pointed in mock surprise, "Jeez, it's the Moon Man!"

"I got wind of some breaking news," Moon Man dashed across the room and took a fistful of undershirt in his left hand, "Now you want to shoot the breeze?"

"Look," Stuart covered his his face as Moon Man raised his fist, "I'll break wind with yah. Just don't break up the joint. This stuff costs money, you know."

"Cough it up!" Moon Man shook Stuart by the shoulders.

"Just don't…" Stuart pointed behind him, "Just don't throw me inta' the phonograph. It's brand new. I just bought it, I swear!"

"No two bit punk gives orders to the Moon Man," Moon Man picked him up by the shoulders and threw him atop the wooden record player. It shattered apart.

"Ahh!" Stuart rolled around in pain and banged a microphone against the floor until it broke. Then, he collapsed in the middle of the splintered furniture.

"Are you okay, Stu?" Moon Man fell down on one knee and spoke much more softly.

"Da-aaady?" a voice called from behind the door.

"Now yah done it, Moon Man," Stuart picked up an old doily that had been on the record player, and wiped some blood from his arm, "Dang it! You gotta be so rough?"

"You know a better way to bust up a mike without giving ourselves away?"

"Everything's fine, honey!" Stuart called out, "Daddy's just visiting. Go back to sleep."

"Can I visit the Man Moon?" the voice said.

"We probably don't have much time," Stuart said to Moon Man. He crawled over to a cabinet and took out a small bread box, "The cops'll probably charge the place now."

"Angel's watching out for me," Moon Man kept his head down.

"That guy's a saint!" Stuart pointed. "He got me enough dough for Mary's doctor bills *and* to fix the window."

"*He* did?"

"You know what I mean," Stuart opened the box. "Sure, I know you done the actual job, but he risks his life out in the open delivering the goods to us folks."

"It's not like I can come out in the open."

"Still and all," Stuart said. "He works for a *cop* for pity's sake. He'd be in all kinds of trouble if his boss found out."

"I won't let that happen," Moon Man said.

"Still and all…"

"Mary's doing better?"

"Yeah," Stuart pulled a baseball sized wooden moon puzzle from the box. "Her cast itches her like crazy, but she's a trooper."

"Mr. Moon?" a dark haired six year old girl in her father's good shirt that she was using as a nightgown, and a plaster cast on her left arm, opened the bedroom door and walked out barefoot and wiping her eyes.

"Watch the splinters," Moon Man said.

"Is Daddy helping you fight the bad guys again?"

"He sure is," Moon Man said.

They all turned to look at the front door as they could hear heavy steps running towards them.

"Here," Stuart tossed the puzzle to Moon Man.

"They're coming!" Angel burst into the room.

Moon Man jumped over and pulled the yellowed blind down to cover the window.

"In here," Stuart motioned the men into the dark bedroom just as the police topped the stairs in the hallway.

"Where'd he go?" a young officer bolted into the room.

"Oh, man!" Stuart placed his bloody arm across his chest and breathed heavily, "He done a number on me, I tell yah!"

"Where did he *go*?" the policeman demanded.

"He flew away," Mary pointed at the ceiling. "He jumped off the roof and flew away."

"He went up!" the officer turned to the hall. "We've got him now. There's no way down without going through us."

The policeman slammed the door shut behind him and leapt up the stairs.

"So what's the story?" Moon Man came back out of the room followed by Angel.

"I'll get the car ready," Angel said. "Don't dawdle."

"It's a setup all along," Stuart reported. "The cops heard the rumor about some old broad finding a clue to a treasure map, and they figured they could trap you at the graveyard or here."

"Well, I haven't escaped yet," Moon Man said.

"I like your moon ball," Mary pointed at the small wooden puzzle in his hand. "It has a hole in it."

"So… What? It was just some rich dame's grave stone?" Stuart said. "You find anything useful?"

"Marge Bendicutt was a founder of Great Town," Moon Man informed. "She got rich writing as a fictional pirate named Split-Hat. She died in 1872. You took a picture of her grave stone." Moon Man pulled a picture from his cowl. "Notice anything wrong?"

"Stuart read the stone in the picture, "Marjory Ann Bendicutt, 4-31-1870, Writer to the End."

"Right."

"1870?" Stuart handed the picture back. "I thought you said she died in 1872."

"I did."

"Okay."

"It's wrong," Moon Man held up the ball. "What's with the Chinese moon puzzle?"

"Yeah, here's where it gets interesting…"

"Footsteps!" Mary cried.

"You good at talking on the run?" Moon Man tucked the puzzle into a small pouch under his cowl.

"Just don't throw me down the stairs again," Stuart sighed.

When Angel screeched the car around to the front of the building, Moon

Man had already descended to the third floor, crashed through a hall window and was rebounding off a large flag pole into he space where the open moon roof of the car would be waiting.

"No way you knew that flag pole would be there," Angel's eyes were wide in surprise.

"I just knew you would be," Stephen removed his helmet and panted slowly. "Drive. I'll explain it all at the base. First get us out of here."

As Angel deftly weaved through the back roads and hidden streets of Great City, Stephen held the moon puzzle up to the side window. He could barely see it in the dark, marked only by the feint yellow glow from the instruments in the front of the car. Here was a new mystery dropped on him. He squinted at the tiny writing on the individual pieces. It didn't appear Chinese. Someone had written letters over some faintly carved symbols. For once, he was following clues rather than planting false ones.

"Let's see if there is any connection," he set the ball on the large table in the center of the room once they were back at headquarters. "Things are starting to come together, but not yet adding up." He pulled the light down closer. "We have a copy of the clue from Bendicutt's book," Stephen tapped the paper with his finger, "so conveniently misplaced for the Moon Man to find."

"While helping found this great Great Town,
I kept a few things for my own.
To find the treasures this town gave,
the clue is hidden at my grave." Angel recited. "It was just a trap set for Moon Man. It's looking like a failed set up. What will they think up next?"

"And we have the photo to match the poem," Stephen held the photo up.

"Except there's no clue on the grave," Angel pointed back to the poem, "just a name and a date and an occupation."

"The police may have used the information to trap me," Stephen unhooked his cape and folded it over his arm, "but the information is real, well, the story is real. I know Mrs. Amsterdam. We helped her when her cat had the infected paws."

"Hands," Angel added.

"Hands?"

"The cat's name was Hands."

"Right. Hands," Stephen said. "If she said she found the original note, I have no doubt she did."

"He had these thumbs," Angel looked down at his own pudgy digits and wiggled his thumbs. "It was the freakiest thing. He would carry stuff around, steal her glasses and stuff."

"Hands?"

"Yeah."

"Guess you could call him a cat burglar."

"Hey, that's pretty good, boss."

"I have one in me occasionally," Stephen looked at Angel but tapped the picture behind him, "but back to the photo."

"You reckon it's a clue?" Angel took Stephen's cloak from him and hung it on a peg on the wall.

"It's wrong," Stephen said. "She didn't die on this date."

"How do you know?"

"I checked it out."

"And now we know why you really went to the library on Tuesday."

"She died in 1872," Stephen looked at the photo closer.

"Well, there were a lot of mistakes back in those days," Angel shrugged. "Could be she thought she was dying and bought the stone, only to kick the bucket a couple of years later."

"I have done some studying on one of our prominent founding mothers," Stephen pushed the light back up and took his house coat from its stand next to his large leather chair. "She was quite the writer. She made a good living at it."

"Split-Hat," Angel commented. "The lads and me used to be the scurvy snake pirate, Split-Hat and his gang! We'd jump in a pile of sticks and pretend it was his torture bay full of snakes."

"She wrote *as* Split-Hat," Stephen searched through his pockets and brought out a box of matches. "Many people didn't even realize the books were written by a woman, and assumed it was the pirate himself penning the fantastic tales. Some even believed the stories were based in truth."

"And that there was a treasure?" Angel chuckled.

Stephen set the matches next to his pipe on a small wooden stand and sat down in his chair. He crossed his legs and leaned forward, resting his elbow on his leg and putting his hand up to his chin.

"You're not smoking," Angel pointed out.

"I'm thinking."

"Yes, I know," Angel straddled a stool and sat next to the large table. "You ain't relaxing. Something's got you flustered. Have anything to do with this?" Angel picked up the moon puzzle and tossed it back and forth in his hands.

"It's wrong," Stephen said. "She couldn't have died then. It's impossible, and it was on purpose."

"How do you gather?" Angel set the ball back down. "Lots of people die everyday. It's always possible."

"Not on this day, Ned," Stephen sat up straight. "Nobody died on this date."

"How can you be sure?"

"April 31st?"

"Yeah."

"There *is* no April 31st, Angel," Stephen smirked. "April only has thirty days."

"Well, I'll be…" Angel jerked his attention over to the photo. "It's wrong on purpose!"

"It's a clue."

"A clue to what?"

"A writer to the end, indeed," Stephen tapped his pipe between his teeth.

"What's wrong?"

"The clue is wrong."

"Come again?" Angel cupped his cauliflower ear.

"She was a writer to the end," Stephen repeated. "She planted the poem inside one of her personal copies of Split-Hat, a copy that would remain in Great City."

"So?"

"So, it was a very specific copy. It was, *Split-Hat's Revenge.*"

"How is that any different than any of the other pirate tales?"

"It was the last pirate tale," Stephen leaned back. "Split-Hat dies at the end."

"*Supposedly* dies!" Angel suggested. "Nobody believed he really died. She just never got a chance to write another one."

"Oh, he died," Stephen puffed the empty pipe, "and Bendicutt wanted to leave some clues. She knew her note would lead to her gravesite…"

"But, it's wrong."

"But, it's wrong," Stephen confirmed. "It's the wrong clue. It's the wrong gravesite. It's the wrong death."

"The wrong death?"

"People thought Bendicutt *was* Split-Hat," Stephen said, "She wrote as Split-Hat. She wasn't talking about her grave. She was talking about *his* grave."

"His ship went down in the fog," Angel said.

"Of Great City Harbor."

"Mills Harbor?" Angel looked over to the window.

""No," Stephen set his pipe back down. "That's our current harbor. In the last century our original harbor silted in. They built Greatway Bridge over it. Marge Bendicutt was a contributor to it. It was one of her final projects for the city."

"Right," Angel said.

"The real Split-Hat was based on an outlaw and a pirate named Archibald Jeffers," Stephen continued. "I need to do some research on him."

"So what about this ball, then?" Angel picked up the puzzle.

She knew her note would lead to her gravesite…

Stephen sighed.

"Something wrong?"

"He says he knows me…" Stephen looked into the dark corners of his study, "from Tuesday to Monday."

"Who?"

"Some elderly British man gave Stuart this puzzle, which at first I thought was Chinese," Stephen nodded towards the wooden ball. "The gentleman knew my working relationship with Mr. Lee, how we acted like he was a crook and let the police and the underground feed him information."

"Lucky guess?" Angel tossed the ball to Stephen who was motioning for it. "It's not impossible to figure out, I suppose."

"That's why I was hesitant to do it in the first place, despite the positive possibilities," Stephen shook his head, "I didn't like endangering Mary."

"She seems like she'll be a fighter," Angel smiled. "She knocked those bullies down a peg."

"And she got her arm broken for it," Stephen cupped the ball in his fingers. "Did you notice the symbols carved into the puzzle?"

"I felt them."

"Each piece of the puzzle has a little unseen symbol carved into the moon," Stephen turned the ball in his hand. "I don't pretend to know what they all mean, but I recognize the days of the week from Evrim's Diner."

"Turkish?"

"Tuesday through Monday, Ned," Stephen looked up as he turned the ball. "There are letters and numbers that someone has written on the face of the moon. At first I thought it was a key on how to solve it, but I realized it was a whole new puzzle."

"What do you mean?" Angel stood up.

"The key to solving the moon puzzle is an actual key," Stephen pointed at a six sided hole in the puzzle. "It goes in this little hole. Without the key, known as the *man in the moon*, you can't open the puzzle."

"Break it open."

""They are traditionally designed to destroy the message if that happens with a dye or an acid," Stephen said. "Look at these letters."

Angel looked at the moon in Stephen's hand, "What does it spell?"

"Follow the week and it spells trouble."

"Trouble?"

"Tuesday is S," Stephen turned the ball. "Wednesday is T. Thursday, Friday, Saturday; E, P, H. Sunday is another E, and Monday…"

"N," Angel caught on. "Tuesday through Monday is, STEPHEN." His jaw dropped.

"They never found Split-Hat's body," Stephen said. "It looks like we're going to have to."

"We're not so smart," Moon Man said as he and Angel stood in the shadows of the dark river bank behind a large broken concrete wall. "We should have come last night when we first figured out the deception."

"The clues have been making the rounds for weeks, boss, but it don't appear they got too far yet," Angel peered through his binoculars at the handful of men in suits and hats who were hacking away the old vines and throwing off discarded trash at the base of a huge support under the Greatway Bridge. One short old man held a lantern up to provide some limited light on this foggy wet September night. What moon there was hid behind clouds. It was about to make an entrance.

"I suppose I should be happy it's not more than just Dumbo's gang," Moon Man whispered. "It could be half the gangs of Great City."

"Or even gangs from other cities," Angel took a deep breath, "by now."

"I'm going to attempt to come in from behind," Moon Man checked his gear. "If I can grab Marcetti, his goons won't risk firing. You come in with the cuffs and lock them down."

"Right," Angel rifled through his black leather bag and pulled out several sets of handcuffs.

As the moon came around out of the clouds, Frank 'Dumbo' Marcetti directed his three large men to continue chopping at the undergrowth. From their matted and bedraggled state, it was evident that they had been at it for some time. This was their third support cleared and the last one that could be reached by land. The men had long since discarded their suit coats and ties, but the humidity and the sweat and the mud and the bugs didn't seem to bother Marcetti as he puffed on a stubby cigar and held up the light. He was still dressed to the nines, standing on his men's coats to avoid sinking into the wet stinking sand and sludge at the water's edge.

There was no wind, so Moon Man had to make his way slowly and arduously through the ten foot tall forest of reeds growing farther back on the banks. A mere two feet from Marcetti, Moon Man hid his large head behind an old river willow that grew crooked out over the water. He reached out with his camouflaged black gloves and nearly had his hands around Marcetti's throat, when the crook turned around and pointed a pistol right at him.

"Don't tell me you thought you could sneak up on *me*," Marcetti tossed his cigar at Moon Man and pointed to his own large ears. "They don't call me Dumbo because I ain't smart!"

"You will rue the day…" Moon Man began in his low voice.

"Yeah, yeah, we'll all rue the day. Get out here," Marcetti motioned with his gun. "You boys rueing the day?"

"I'm rueing the night right now, boss," one of the thugs massaged a blister on his thumb. "But I think we mighta' found something."

"Yeah? Well, open it up, fellas," Marcetti motioned again for Moon Man to move. "Better yet, let's let our mystery-man here do it. He's gotta be good for something, on accounta' what I heard, he's hated by both sides of the law."

As Moon Man walked by Marcetti, he stomped down hard on the suit coats and drove them into the sand. Marcetti nearly fell, and had to catch himself. At that moment, Moon Man grabbed his gun hand and twisted it around his back, forcing him to drop the weapon. Moon Man scooped it up and held it to Marcetti's head.

"Get back!" Moon Man ordered.

"You idiot!" Marcetti snapped. "There's no way you can shoot alla' my boys before they plug you, and I don't buy fer one minute that yer bulletproof or you wouldn't a' bothered with me."

"I thought your ears were big," Moon Man put the end of the pistol inside Marcetti's ear. "But your mouth is even bigger."

Bang! A shot fired from the wooded area. The slug hit Moon Man in the head and knocked him back just a step. It was enough for Marcetti to grab his gun back and to push away. Moon Man took a knee to the sand as Marcetti's men started firing into the blackness over to their right from where the shot had come. Moon Man whipped out his own .45 and held it up.

"Stop!" he ordered.

The men pointed their guns at Moon Man.

"We ain't the only ones what figured it out," Marcetti stood behind one of his men and straightened his tie. "The more time we waste out here in the open, the more knobs we'll have to mess with later."

"I suggest you stand down then," Moon Man searched the darkness for Angel. "That treasure can help a lot of people."

"I suggest we split it," Marcetti held up his lantern. "We keep our streets safe and clean, and most of what you stupidly dole out ends up back in our hands anyway. You just save a few knuckleheads a broken hand or a smashed up store front."

"It really doesn't matter what you suggest," a ghostly figure of a man shimmered above the ground to the left of the group. It was a man in a bluish suit and tie. He had a sharp little goatee and a fedora and a black mask that covered the top half of his face.

"Holy smokes, it's a ghost!" one of the men shouted.

The three thugs all began firing at the figure. Moon Man dove back behind the river willow, and Marcetti threw himself against the recently uncovered stone doorway, opening it just a crack.

"The whole treasure will be mine, anyways," the ghostly man smiled and floated towards them. The bullets passed harmlessly through him, "None of you even really matter. If it wasn't for me, there wouldn't even *be* a treasure."

"He's a ghost! A *ghost!*"

"The slugs go right through him!"

"What'll we do, boss?"

"I don't care what he is," Marcetti pushed against the door. "He ain't got a piece. He can't hurt you. Now get over here and help me open this thing up."

"Oh, now that is where you are wrong, indistinct criminal representation," the ghost pointed a finger at one of the men. "*Bang,*" he said.

A second later a shot rang out from the distance. The bullet struck Marcetti's largest man directly in the head. He fell over dead into the muck.

"Wow!" the ghost looked at his gun fingers in surprise. "I'm *amazing!*"

"Aaah!" the other men screamed and slammed themselves into the heavy concrete door.

The door swung back and banged into a wall behind it. The three men fell inside and nearly doused the lantern. Without pause, they jumped up and continued down a winding spiral staircase as fast as they could move.

"Good Lord!" Moon Man gasped.

The ghost swung his gaze in Moon Man's direction. He floated up to the tree.

"What are you waiting for, Moon Man?" the ghost smiled at him. "Go get my treasure. I don't have all night. Well, I *do*, but only just."

"What are you?" Moon Man looked up at the figure.

"I'm everything," the ghost grinned, "but you can call me the Dream Man if it helps. This should be fun. I've never had a treasure hunt dream before."

"Fun?" Moon Man stepped out from behind the tree. "You shot that man in cold blood."

"Please," the Dream Man waved his hand. "He can't have been *that* important. His name wasn't revealed. He didn't have any outstanding or interesting traits that added to the story. The only importance he had to the narrative was to die."

"He probably had a family or loved ones," Moon Man pointed at the dead man.

"No," the Dream Man raised a ghostly eyebrow. "He didn't, and neither will you if you don't go get my treasure. I'll be in shortly."

Moon Man stood straight and peered into the darkness. The Dream Man pointed his forefinger at Moon Man's heart.

"Ka-*click*..." the Dream Man cocked his thumb.

Without a word, Moon Man entered the small room inside the pillar and descended the stairs inside. He withdrew his flashlight to give him some sense of his environment. River water washed away a small sand dam at the doorway and immediately began flooding into the rusty stairwell as soon as the door was unsealed. He wasn't sure just how long he had until the whole thing was flooded. The stream wasn't overwhelming, but it was gradually increasing. Slime covered the walls and dripped down from the ceiling as the stairwell opened up into a larger room. In the center of the room there were small pipes at the floor level that ran black water in open troughs across the floor. The small troughs, in turn, ran into three different tunnels in front of him. This must have been some early sewage system for the town. Cobwebs covered two of the tunnel entrances, leaving an obvious path as to where Marcetti and his men had gone. The running water made it difficult to hear, but he was certain that was the tunnel they took. There were still dry paths on the floor along the sides of the troughs. The water flooding in still filled the trenches for now. If there was a natural or constructed exit still available for all this water, the tunnels would be fine, but if it had been sealed up, any long lost pirate or treasure might be sealed up with it. He started to take the tunnel after Marcetti, when a bright light flooded the room behind him.

"I wonder what you are?" the Dream Man shone a large hand held spotlight in one hand and held a gun in the other. He looked much less ghostly than before and he wasn't floating. He had a rifle with a scope strapped to his back, "Come back here and let me get a better look at you. That's the wrong way, anyways."

"How do you know?" Moon Man took a couple of steps back.

"That's the way Marcetti went," the Dream Man shone his light around at the other tunnels. "The story wouldn't make much sense if *he* found the treasure."

"What story?"

"You see, Marcetti represents a barrier I need to overcome," the Dream Man stepped closer to Moon Man, "maybe a physical restriction, maybe some ethical hurdle..."

"Maybe mental," Moon Man sloshed to the middle of the room.

"Could be, could be," the Dream Man rubbed his chin. "Anyways, we take this one."

"We?" Moon Man looked at the middle passage where the Dream Man had the light. "And how can *we* be sure?"

Because it's my dream," the Dream Man cleared some cobwebs with his light. "I always find the treasure in my dreams. I always win… usually. It wouldn't make sense otherwise."

"Because it's making so much sense right now," Moon Man cleared a different tunnel with his own small light. "I think I'll take this way."

"No, I think your part in the dream must be over," the Dream Man pulled his rifle from behind his back in one smooth practiced motion. "I'm going to shoot the moon!"

Before the Dream Man could act, Moon Man tumbled forward and threw his flashlight at the Dream Man's head. The light spun in a dizzying arc that both blinded and disoriented him. Moon Man ducked as he somersaulted over a trench, jumped back up in front of the Dream Man, hitting him hard in the chin with the top of his Argus helmet. The Dream Man fell backwards into the shallow water. His rifle skitted across a dry patch, out of reach. Both men immediately flipped back up off their backs. The Dream Man wiped blood from the corner of his mouth and fairly fell towards Moon Man. The figures wrestled in the near dark like two entwined snakes trying desperately to both choke the life out of each other and escape the suffocating embrace.

"Just who do you think you are?" the Dream Man screamed at his dim distorted reflection in Moon Man's helmet. "Shut up! No, *you* shut up! Don't yell at me! I'll kill you! No, I'll kill you!"

Moon Man brought his knee up and pushed the Dream Man back. The Dream Man tripped on the edge of a trench and fell over backwards, just as Moon Man managed to pull out his own .45.

"Now…" Moon Man pointed the weapon.

The Dream Man kicked the gun from Moon Man's hand. It plopped down into the brackish water of a narrow trench. Moon Man whipped around and ran to the base of the stairs, only to be stopped by the shot from a gun. The bullet hit him in the helmet and ricocheted down to the metal banister, slicing open the back of his black glove and creasing a layer of skin from his wrist down the back of his hand in between his first and second knuckle.

"Sssss…!" Moon Man grabbed his left hand in his right.

"Don't move, Moon Man," the Dream Man had his rifle and his powerful flashlight trained on Moon Man.

Moon Man raised his hands and turned around. Blood from his wound ran down his arm and mingled with the sweat and sewage and filth.

"Who are you?" the Dream Man said again, and stepped up to Moon Man.

"It doesn't matter," Moon Man replied.

"You must be someone from my life," the Dream Man stepped forward, nearly slipping. "They always are when they have a big role."

"From your life?"

"My eighth grade teacher?" the Dream Man examined Moon Man. "No, she was a woman. A childhood friend? A fellow soldier? Take off the helmet. I'm ready."

"No," Moon Man said.

"I could take it off your corpse," the Dream Man raised his gun and light. "Maybe that would teach me something."

"You would shoot your, uh... mailman?" Moon Man stepped up very close. The gun pressed against his chest where he held the ball puzzle in a pouch.

"Moon Man is mailman?" the Dream Man turned his head slightly in thought. "Mr. Miller... Mr. Mervine Miller...?"

"Yes, Miller," Moon Man urged. "You found me out."

"It all makes sense now," the Dream Man looked away, "the missing milk on Mondays, Mervine Miller, milkman, Moon Man..."

Moon Man twisted in a quick jerk, flinging his cape as he knocked the gun away with his left hand and grabbed the Dream Man's mask with his right.

"Aaah!" the Dream Man screamed and fired a shot into the wall. He hunched over and pulled his mask all the way off so he could see.

Moon Man was shocked to see the Dream Man's face as he rose back up. The skin around his eyes was heavily scarred from what must have been burns, and his eyebrows were missing.

"Don't look at me!" the Dream Man swung wildly with the butt of his rifle and struck Moon Man in the helmet.

Moon Man fell backwards a step, and the Dream Man leapt upon him, pinning him to the wall.

"I see you! I see you!" the Dream Man poked his finger against his own reflection. "Now I get it! Now I *know!*"

Moon Man remained silent, not even struggling against the mad man's grip.

"Why do you look like this, too? How did you get those scars?" the Dream Man drew his face so close to Moon Man's helmet that his nose was touching it, "Right? *Right?*"

"I just..." Moon Man said.

"Quiet!" the Dream Man spat on the helmet as he screamed. "I wasn't talking to *you!* I was talking to the listeners."

"I'm... listening," Moon Man stated.

"Pierce Newman faced a dare to spend the night in the most haunted place on earth," the Dream Man said, "the decrepit old mansion known as the House of Spades. Little did he realize what evil..."

The Dream Man stopped. He pulled back and pointed his gun at Moon man. His eyes searched in his head. "No," he said.

Moon Man raised his hands.

The Dream Man reached over and wiped at his funhouse reflection in Moon Man's head. "No," he said again. "Wrong story. You deserve the truth. The moon deserves the truth, especially you."

Moon Man looked over in the darkness for his submerged gun.

"I can see the pain in your eyes," the Dream Man searched his own reflection, "the pain and confusion. I feel your pain, Moon Man, but this is all your fault. You sent this down on me."

"How can you say…?"

"It was coming right at me, right for me," the Dream Man aimed his gun at Moon Man's head, "the fire from the sky aimed at the best sharp shooter in the country. There was Newman Pierce, a sharpshooter for the US Cavalry, on a grassy hillside, aiming down, preparing to shoot his… the government's target. Then, out of the sky came a flaming ball."

"A meteor?"

"I used to think it came from Heaven," the Dream Man said, "that it was the answer to my prayers not to have to take the shot, but now I know…"

The Dream Man gazed at Moon Man, "It came from the moon…"

The Dream Man petted Moon Man on his wet dome, "and I shot it into a million pieces, a million blazing shards that filled the countryside and my targets and my face."

He lowered his gun and pulled a thin sheet of milky white stone from his pocket. It had been cut into a sharp triangle about three inches on all sides and a half inch thick. He popped it into a slot in his special flashlight, and turned a knob with his thumb. He pointed the light at himself, and a ghostly replica appeared on the far wall. The more he rotated the dial, the closer and farther the figure floated. Whatever move he made, the ghost made.

"Moon magic," he said. "You see how the answers all come to me in my dream?"

"That sounds… impossible," Moon Man argued.

"You don't get to tell me what's impossible!" the Dream Man hissed, and then smiled, "Everything is possible in my dream, in my story."

"Now that you have your answers," Moon Man scooted along the wall towards the first tunnel, "perhaps I should be going."

"This magic moon mineral has made me," the Dream Man and his ghost raised their arms. "But perhaps you are right." He popped the stone out of the light, and his spirit vanished, "This could merely be my subconscious exploring different routes, trying new things. They say that everyone in a dream is you.

Perhaps you are me, as well."

"Whatever helps you sleep," Moon Man stepped into the black slimy tunnel.

"Heh, that's funny," the Dream Man flung his gun back over his shoulder. "No, wait, I know! You represent the *wrong* choice. You'll reach a dead end, and I'll find your horribly mutilated body caught in some arcane trap."

Moon Man could still hear the Dream Man talking to himself for a few minutes as he walked down the canal. The tunnel gradually got smaller and shorter. Soon, he was hunched over, then down on his hands and knees. Still, he kept going past multiple side doors. He followed straight ahead, figuring he could always double back to one of the doors. As the hall graduated to where he had to crawl on his belly, he decided to turn around. At the edge of his light, though, was one more small door. It was a round hatch that opened to the right just as the hallway ended. His Argus helmet scraped the sides as he wedged himself forward, holding his light out ahead. He was sure at that point that he would not turn around; mainly because he was sure he *could* not turn around if he wanted. He could no longer push back against the wet walls. He either moved forward, or he never moved again. The walls closed around his shoulders as he reached the final portal.

"Ugh! This had better… lead to someplace, or I might just never… get…" he spoke to himself as he twisted the rusty handle and pushed the portal door open away from him.

He could see a flickering light beyond as he wormed his way ninety degrees through the hole. He slammed his head against the opening three times before his helmet went through. He didn't really fit through the space, but he was determined to force himself out of the claustrophobic confines he was in. Fortunately, the hole opened up into quite a large room. He was in the top of the wall near the ceiling where the opening was hidden well by the spiders and the shadows. Emerging from the tunnel, the reflection from his helmet glinting off the flickering firelight, he looked like the moon trying desperately to peer beneath the clouds and the forest canopy, albeit a grunting, jerking moon, wet with dank water and hoping not to get stuck and die in a sewer. He plopped from the tunnel like a torn cork, flipped in the air to land on his feet fifteen feet below. His feet hit solid, but the wetness of everything made him slip and fall on his backside. The moon puzzle jumped up out of his pocket, and he caught it in his bloody hands.

"Back you go," he tucked it into his breast pocket.

Across the large room was another open portal, this one as large as a standard door. A torch had been lit, but was lying on the ground near a stream of water in the middle of the floor. It spat and hissed in the dampness. Aside from three smaller tubes that took the runoff, the tunnel ended in a large wall

"This had better...lead to someplace..."

to his left. The dark to his right must have been where Marcetti or the Dream Man had come... unless there were already new actors at play.

Moon Man hopped over the stream and picked up the old torch. Its flame had died down to a blue wisp around the wick. It provided enough light, though that he was able to turn off his flashlight to conserve the battery. He hooked it on his belt and continued on. The big square room led into an oval brick tunnel beyond. He stepped up into the dryer curved room and had to find his footing. The floor was as circular as the walls, and it was difficult to walk. When the gunshots in the distance began, however, he started to sprint.

Before he reached the yellow glow a hundred yards down the long tunnel, the shots stopped. All was quiet as he reached the distant open oval door. He stopped short and backed against the wall of the opening. He clicked his helmet to the side and took it off. The air was no less foul than what had been filtering in through his headpiece, but it let him glance out into the room without being obvious. The carnage he saw beyond made him bite his lip in order to silence the gasp that tried so desperately to escape. The Dream Man was down below in a large square room. He had the dead body of Marcetti in one hand and his rifle pointed at Marcetti's head in the other. He held Marcetti by the lapels and spoke to him. Marcetti's other two men were lying on either side. They were not breathing. Blood ran from all four men and drained into the multiple small canals criss-crossing the floor. Two torches lay on slightly raised walks and art least one more torch was in the gutter.

"You see..." the Dream Man huffed in pain, "It's not always easy, you see... huhh, huhhh..."

He dropped Marcetti face first into a stream of foamy black water mingled with his own blood. Then, he slung his rifle back over his shoulder and winced in pain. Blood stained the left sleeve of his jacket, up close to his shoulder. Even from his vantage point, Moon Man could see the tear in the clothes where the bullet had exited.

"This must be..." the Dream Man walked in a small circle and addressed the dead men, "I figure this must be... The pain, you see, is probably a symbol of... the daily struggle to..."

Moon Man reaffixed his helmet and stepped into the room. He raised his torch above his head, "You killed them all!"

"Back in Veil City," the Dream Man stepped back in surprise. "I used to have this same problem. The local masked hero..." The Dream Man cleared his throat and shook himself. "I *dreamed* I had this problem, I mean. Slipknot thought I was... He thought maybe I should take a vacation..."

"You should be in the electric chair!" Moon Man leapt across the dead men directly into the Dream Man.

Moon Man's torch fell into the water and went out. Only one single torch on the damp floor lit the ensuing melee. The other was nearly out as well. "I'd have been dead too if my helmet hadn't deflected the shot outside," Moon Man knocked the Dream Man over on his back and blocked the rifle butt coming at him in response.

"I didn't… mmph!" the Dream Man lost his gun and attempted to rock his way out from under the weight of the Moon Man's body.

The two men rolled around in the filth and the blood and the water and the dead, punching and pulling. Moon Man had the upper hand with his protective helmet, but the Dream Man was more athletically built and had greater reach, even with his injury.

Bang!

Zing!

The Dream Man shot Moon Man in the head at close range with a pistol he pulled out of his jacket. The bullet ricocheted into Marcetti's body.

"You can't ruin my story!" the Dream Man cried. "I win! *I* win!"

Moon Man fell against the Dream Man's arm, his elbow pressing hard against the Dream Man's wrist. The gun fell away, and Moon Man staggered up. The Dream Man leapt up with a crazed fury, and lunged at Moon Man. Moon Man countered with a fist to the Dream Man's right cheek.

"Ufph!" the Dream Man spit.

"You will *not* win!" Moon Man hit him in the gut with his bloody fist.

"Hoof!"

"You will *not* get the treasure!" Moon Man leaned into a hard left uppercut into the Dream Man's chin.

"Akk!"

"Because *this*…" a crossover right into the Dream Man's right temple, "…is…"

"Buhhh!"

"*Not…!*" a knee to the groin.

"Your…" an elbow between the eyes.

The two men stood in front of each other. Moon Man huffed, and the Dream Man wobbled in a daze. Moon Man picked up the dead torch from the water. He swung it around with both hands in a low rising arc, and connected with the Dream Man's face.

"…*Story!*"

The Dream Man toppled immediately. He popped down to the wet gritty floor and didn't move. He barely breathed. Moon Man pulled any weapon off of him that he could find and tossed it in the water. He found the Dream Man's flashlight and flipped it on. The lens was cracked, but it still worked. He couldn't find the strange stone.

He caught his breath and looked around. He could see down the passage a ways where Marcetti and his men had entered. He saw a separate tunnel where the Dream Man had come in. The water again exited through small pipes. Only upon closer inspection did he notice the rusty ladder in the corner leading up to a square alcove above.

"Better not be another tiny tunnel," he said, "or I'm just going home. Treasure be damned."

Someone else had been to the ladder before him. The prints in the slime attested to one other person who was recently here. Moon Man took a final look around at the crazy and the dead, and started up the cold steel ladder. His hands ached with every rung. Even through his gloves, he had bruised his knuckles, and his bullet injury was swelling quite a bit. When he topped the climb, there was a small square room about ten feet tall. A steel door was ajar in the far wall. He sat at the ledge and draped one foot over. He twisted his helmet off and removed it, breathing in the sickly stale air as if it were a mountain breeze. He took off one glove and attempted to wipe the sweat out of his eyes, but it just stung all the more. After a minute, he spat, stood and reattached his helmet. He forced his wet glove over his sore pruney hands and walked towards the door.

"Hello, Stephen," a voice said from the room on the other side. "I've been waiting for you."

A man stood close to the middle of what felt like a large, low ceiling room. Moon Man couldn't see all around the dark area. The old man was illuminated by a small square gas lantern in his hand, but the circle of light around him only stretched out so far.

"The mystery man," Moon Man stood in the doorway. "I'm really not in the mood."

"I expect not, if all has gone to prediction," the man pointed at the floor in between them. "You might consider where you step before you enter."

Moon Man shone his light across the floor. He twisted the top of the flashlight and it clicked brighter. Hundreds of sparkling glass marbles glimmered in square stone tiles. It was like a sky full of stars.

"More like an ocean," the old man said, predicting Moon Man's thoughts, "reflecting the moon off a calm sea. Note the waves in the tiles."

"How do you know me?" Moon Man shone his light at the little old man in the wrinkled brown suit.

"There is a poem," the man shielded his eyes. "It's quite long and rambling, but reasonably sound. It follows the exploits of Captain Split-Hat on his journey through the Veil of Stars."

"Where he's stuck in the Sargasso. I remember," Moon Man lowered his light and began to take a step.

"Wait!" the old man commanded with full British accent and authority. "That would be quite the mistake, dear boy."

"You're talking, but you're not saying anything," Moon Man never-the-less stood still. "Is that a coffin?"

The old man turned his light on to a rectangular stone box in the very center of the room. It had fairly plain sides, but the stone lid was highly decorated with a relief of a man in the center of the top.

"More of a sarcophagus," he said. "However, we must take great care in approaching it."

"Booby traps?"

"And false clues," the man looked down at his feet. He was standing on a square that was an inch lower than all the tiles around. "I followed the Veil of Stars religiously. If you note the arrangements of the glass in the floor. The constellations are spelled out along a crooked path. They follow their mention and his journey in the poem."

"Hmmm..." Moon Man squatted down and examined the marbles. "You traveled the same path that took Spit-Hat to Devil Island?"

"Given the set up of the stones, it seemed an obvious clue," the man said. "But it was a trick."

"How so?"

"I could not see the Devil himself," the man raised his lantern and pointed across the room, "the Tempter, the Liar, the Serpent in the Garden..."

"The Snake," Moon Man shone his powerful light over to the wall. Dozens of small snakes were carved in the gray plaster. They were crawling out of holes drilled into the wall.

"Man's weakness has always led him to be blind to the Old Dragon's lies," the man shook his head. "My weakness is my eyesight and my age. I have found that a lot of my keen sight in a lot of different ways has waned with the years."

"So... snakes?" Moon Man turned to the opposite wall and found it was also covered in snakes. "Surely that's not very plausible. How can the trap be snakes? Wouldn't they need to be kept alive somehow over the years?"

"The poem lied," the man said. "I stepped in accordance with the verse, but my final footfall caused this tile to release. I fear my weight is the only thing keeping me alive."

"I don't get it," Moon Man stepped into the room, following the constellations in the poem that he and every school child in Great City learned in grade school. "I thought Split-Hat tamed the snakes."

"Tamed means killed," the man followed Moon Man's steps with care. "He tamed them with stick and spear..."

"What next?" Moon Man looked at the slabs in front of him. "Was it...?"

"Cancer."

"Right," Moon Man took a step and quoted, "Into the Tropic of the Great Crab..."

"Now stop," the old man said as they stood side by side.

"The next step..."

"Should be here," the man pointed down, "but it is not. When Split-Hat and his men were surrounded by snakes, they sought refuge on a large rock."

"And fought them off," Moon Man added.

They both turned their lights to the center of the room just a few feet away. The sarcophagus was in the middle of a concrete circle that acted as a pathway all around it.

"You need to get me there," the man said, "in one fell swoop. I knew I would have need of your strength, but I thought it would be for other purposes."

"My strength?"

"Get me to the body of Archibald Jeffers," the man pointed. "Take me to Captain Split-Hat and I will explain further."

"This may prove difficult," Moon Man held out his bloody sore hands.

"Nonsense," the old fellow chuckled. "I chose you very specifically. Step over here."

"You...?" Moon Man stood up against the man on the same tile as him.

"Now, fly!" the old man commanded.

Moon Man reached under the old man's arms and picked him up. He was surprised how light the man was. The old man shut off his lantern. Moon Man jumped as hard as he could towards the center of the room. Even as he did so, he could hear the walls crumbling all around them.

"Good Lord!" Moon Man fell to the large circular slab with his companion still in his arms. The entire room was suddenly filled with arrows. They fired through the holes in the walls, even as those walls were cracking and crumbling. They shot through the billowing dust and traveled the complete distance across the room. Anyone in their path was doomed, unless they were in the one spot that was safe, the sarcophagus and the surrounding circle slab of cold concrete.

The senior treasure hunter coughed. The filters in Moon Man's helmet allowed him to breathe, but he was concerned they might clog. As the dust died down, the old man once again lit his lantern with some matches from a small metal cigarette case. Once they felt it was safe and that no other deadly objects would be hurled in their direction, they stood. They shone their lights out at the walls. Rubble covered the floor along with hundreds of primitive black arrows, sharp sticks all over the floor.

"Snakes," stated the man.

"Overkill," Moon Man said.

"Thankfully not. Look."

Behind where the plaster walls had stood were large passages with curved ceilings. The men turned full circle and counted the many openings around the room.

"Twelve."

"Is that significant to the poem?" Moon Man tried to see down a passage.

"We're beyond the poem now," the old geezer stepped up to the sarcophagus. "We're in a different realm altogether."

"Now you explain," Moon Man followed, "starting with who you are."

"I am a great detective," the man wiped dust from the face of the lid, "the greatest detective of all time."

"That's quite a claim."

"It is not hyperbole if it is true," the man smiled.

"You can't be as great as..."

"Ah. Ah. Ah..." the aged fellow raised a finger. "Would you be the equal of yourself? Would you be the greater?"

"But he is dead."

"Let us leave it that way, then. Shall we?" the man waved over his shoulder. "My name would only muddle the situation. I am not here officially, in any case. That would be treason. Refer to me only as Brown, Mr. Brown."

Mr. Brown pushed on the lid, but Moon Man took hold of his arm and stopped him.

"How do you know me?" Moon man asked. "That much is very important. Lives could be at stake."

"I study all the American masked men," Mr. Brown turned and looked into Moon Man's helmet. "It is a hobby of mine, you see. I'm familiar with dozens of you vigilantes who claim varying degrees of goodness and badness in and outside the law. Whether they be operatives in New York or Great City or Yorktown or Veil City, or any number of your urban aeries, I know their names and operations. It does not suit me to reveal them to anyone, and it never will."

That's very dangerous knowledge," Moon Man stood over Mr. Brown.

"Are you going to murder me, Mr. Thatcher?" Mr. Brown held his lantern up to Moon man's helmet. "I have no need for blackmail, and I never would have revealed myself to you had I not known your penchant for not killing. Neither of us is in any danger from the other."

"How do I know? How can I trust you?"

"Is my word not good enough for you?" Brown reached up and drew a smile on Moon Man's helmet in the dust. "I am intimately familiar with death. You might say it is my middle name."

"The Serpent in the Garden," Moon Man shone his light on the stone lid. "We had nothing to fear from it either, nothing but forbidden knowledge and words. It gave us its word, and you can see how *that* worked out."

Mr. Brown shrugged.

"Should we open the casket?" Moon Man suggested after a pause.

"You brought the moon puzzle, I assume?" Mr. Brown held out his hand.

"What is the purpose of this?" Moon Man gritted his teeth and dug the ball out of his pocket.

"Just a test, really," Mr. Brown explained. "I needed to get you here, so I let you know I knew your secrets. I couldn't rely on your greed. Your method of operations doesn't lend itself to greed. You give things away. Undoubtedly you require the funds to so progress, however, I could not sustain on that impetus alone. I scheduled the others accordingly."

Moon Man rolled the moon puzzle around in his hand in front of his face. "You won't mind, then, if it's not important, if I just keep it?" He stuck it back in his pocket.

Mr. Brown looked at him.

"What do you mean by, you scheduled the others?" Moon Man inquired.

Mr. Brown pulled a damp envelope out of his vest pocket. "Do you think this treasure has been a complete secret for more than five decades?"

"The clue was *just* found in…"

"That is only part of the clue," Mr. Brown slid a dark paper from the envelope, "a very important part, a *key* part, mind you, but only a part. I and others have had knowledge of the treasure for quite some time, but not enough of the puzzle to properly suss out its location. Mrs. Bendicutt kept more than one library, you know."

"What do you mean?"

"She had a copy in London," Mr. Brown put on his spectacles and squinted in the dark room at the paper in front of his face. "Just to show we're all chums here, I'll read this off."

"We're all chums?" Moon Man stepped around to see the paper from over Mr. Brown's shoulder. "Are we splitting the treasure?"

"Oh, dear Heavens, no," Mr. Brown smiled. "You will be volunteering your half to me after you have helped me to attain it."

"I think you're…"

"Midnight, midday, less half past three, the Vaulted Hero is the key," Mr. Brown read. "The drawing below is the map to this room from an entrance that was never revealed until your clue surfaced."

Moon Man took the paper and reread the text, "It's a clue, but to what?"

"You see," Mr. Brown turned and leaned against the stone, facing Moon Man. "It is a map and a clue, but it has no key, no starting point, no definition. Your clue was the key, but you weren't the only one to figure it out."

"Marcetti…"

"And the delightfully insane Dream Man," Mr. Brown said, "and seven other individuals of interest. I had to take action."

"By doing what?" Moon Man handed back the paper.

"By creating diversions," Mr. Brown folded the page and put it back in the envelope, then in his pocket. "I deployed operatives to delay a whole host of parties. I know a lot of things about a lot of people. I arranged accidents and red herrings. I even set up a date for two of them. I believe they are getting engaged."

"All to get me here?" Moon Man crossed his arms. "Why let Marcetti and the Dream Man in?"

"To slow you down."

"To…" Moon Man put his hands on his helmet and leaned forward. "You *do* realize that people died here!"

Mr. Brown pursed his lips and looked away.

"Your manipulations killed people," Moon Man towered over Brown. "The great detective I've heard about would never have done that."

"I had to get in here," Mr. Brown said. "I had to get past you lot."

"I don't think I'll be giving you *any* of the treasure."

"This treasure will free hundreds of thousands," Mr. Brown turned to the sarcophagus. "It will aid in breaking tyranny and slavery. Possibly millions will be given a better life with its aid. Can any of your petty thefts accomplish such a task?"

"How can a treasure, even a large one, do all that?"

"I think it's a clock," Mr. Brown pushed on the lid, but nothing happened.

"The treasure is a clock?"

"The room is a clock," Mr. Brown picked up his lantern and turned around the room slowly. "See the twelve evenly spaced doors? See the sarcophagus pointing north to twelve?"

"Like a clock," Moon Man shone his light into the black tunnel. "Midnight."

"Exactly."

"Then, midday…" Moon Man pointed his light in the opposite direction.

"Is the exact same," Mr. Brown reached over and lowered Moon Man's flashlight.

"It would be, wouldn't it?"

"I believe we're on a fulcrum," Mr. Brown cast his light on the floor. "If so, we can turn this casket all the way around."

"Clockwise?" Moon Man said.

"But of course," Mr. Brown leaned against the stone, "with your necessary assistance."

"Surely it's too heavy to…" Moon Man was astonished as the entire vault turned with their effort. Something below them clicked as they moved. Once it spun one complete circle, it popped and locked in place.

"That was a correct move," Mr. Brown looked around the room and up at the ceiling. "We have not been assailed by projectiles, at any rate."

"Mmmph!" Moon Man pushed. "It won't turn anymore, though. How do we get it to half past three?"

"*Less* half past three," Mr. Brown raised a finger.

"Backwards!" Moon Man walked around to the other side.

"That's how I read it," Mr. Brown joined him and began to push.

When the crypt reached the point where it pointed between doors three and four, it popped and locked again. Other sounds of levers and weights and chains clanked throughout the room. Both men searched the darkness for danger or answers. Two iron spikes knocked a large concrete brick from the wall between doors three and four, revealing a small alcove inside of it. The men approached the space that was two foot square and about five feet off the floor. On a small wooden shelf inside was a small copper box that was decorated with the moon and stars.

"The Vaulted Hero is the key," Mr. Brown stuck his hand in and brought out the box.

"That's not all," Moon Man shone his light in the hole to reveal an iron handle at the top of a long round shaft that extended into the darkness. "I'm not so sure we should turn it."

"Even if you do not trust me," Mr. Brown opened the box, "now is the time for you to hand over the puzzle."

"Why?"

Mr. Brown brought forth an oddly shaped key from the box, "Because I have the man in the moon."

"Tell me first," Moon Man reached into his pocket with his good hand. "Where did you get this puzzle?"

"It is from royalty, my boy," Mr. Brown held out his hand. "It was held once in the chambers of the Dinjabi treasure room."

"The Turkish country?"

"The British colony," Mr. Brown exchanged the box with the puzzle from Moon Man. "Once a small but proud nation, Dinjab fell to tea and the British

"Where did you get this puzzle?"

navy fifty years ago. Its royal family was welcomed into a kept life in London."

"What became of the treasure, then?" Moon Man wanted to know. "The royal family used it to live on?"

"Mostly, yes," Mr. Brown slid the key into the puzzle. It fit perfectly. "Some was taken by the Brits, of course, and some…" The puzzle bloomed open in Mr. Brown's hand, "Some was stolen by pirates."

"By *a* pirate," Moon Man glanced at the vault.

"Indeed," Mr. Brown lifted a small rolled paper from the puzzle. "Our own, Captain Jeffers, the infamous Split-Hat."

Moon Man held a light on the paper as Mr. Brown set the puzzle remains on the floor and unrolled the waxy dark clue.

"How many more clues are there?" Moon Man asked.

"This would typically be the last," Mr. Brown squinted over his glasses. "A trusted ally or the king himself often held this final piece. Although at times, even a princess might have it."

"The Ultimate Passion of Woes protects the moon and holds it down," Moon Man read over Mr. Brown's shoulder. "What does it mean?"

"It means we have to turn the lever," Mr. Brown stroked his chin.

"I don't think the tricks are over," Moon Man warned. "Remember that the other clue lied."

"All clues lie to some degree or other," Mr. Brown set his lantern and the clue on the floor next to the puzzle. He reached with both hands into the alcove and took hold of the iron handle. "It's just… umf! how much we want to believe they are true that… mmm-matters."

He stepped back, "No dice, old boy. I'm afraid it's up to you. These old bones harbor no lies about their failing strength, I'll tell you that."

Moon Man took a deep breath and tucked his flashlight under his arm. He reached his sorry shaking bleeding hands into the hole and grasped the smooth cold metal. He grunted and turned at the handle to no avail.

"Gah!" he pulled back and held out his hands in angry trembling claws. Blood dripped to the floor.

"Try clockwise…"

"I *am* trying clockwise!" Moon Man shouted.

Undeterred, Mr. Barton picked up his lantern and held it to his stony but wrinkled face. "Then, try counter clockwise," he said simply.

"I…" Moon Man made fists and regretted it. He turned back to the alcove and inserted his hands. He breathed heavily twice, then put his full strength into the task.

With a raking rasp, the handle turned. Moon Man cried out in pain and exertion. His flashlight fell to the floor, but stayed lit.

"Aaaah!" he screamed as the entire room shook. Huge slabs of oak fell down over the doors one by one. They were strapped together with broad iron and nails.

Mr. Brown fell down into the rising dust as the room quaked.

"No!" Moon Man ran to a doorway just as the exit was lost. "No!"

He fell to his knees amongst the rubble and the sticks, "I told you! I *told* you!"

For a few minutes after the calamity, all was silent. The dust didn't settle as quickly as before, and hung as an oppressive part of the darkness. Moon Man closed his eyes and laid his injured hands palm up on the floor. He breathed intentionally, in an effort to calm himself and to mute the pain. Two lights approached him from behind.

"Get up," Mr. Brown placed the flashlight next to Moon Man. "Your part is not yet over."

"My *part...*" Moon Man looked over at his light.

"There is an uprising," Mr. Brown's knees clicked as he squatted down next to Moon Man. "The royal family is trying to take back their country from the occupiers. The Dinjabi people want their freedom, a representative democracy run by a parliament, but with a symbolic royal family."

"Let them eat cake," Moon Man admonished.

"That makes no sense," Mr. Brown grunted as he stood back up.

"None of this makes any sense," Moon Man picked up his light.

"Surely an American can relate to wanting to break the shackles of tyranny," Mr. Brown said, "to crack the yoke of oppression and proclaim autonomy."

"And just how will we be able to do that when we're stuck at the bottom of a sewer?"

"The treasure would be a good start," Mr. Brown said. "Gold and jewels can buy a lot, and can also focus and foster a feeling of patriotism to rally a people. Mostly, though, I am hoping for the Crescent Moon."

"The moon?" Moon Man looked up.

"You see, symbols are important to this sort of thing," Mr. Brown held out his hand. "Did you think I only needed your young muscles to achieve my goal? I could have hired any thuggish peon for that task. The Crescent Moon Diamond is the greatest gem of the Dinjabi Empire. It has been a part of the dynasty for a thousand years with magical properties and heroic tales. At least, that is the story, and without the story, where would any of us be? The Ultimate Passion of Woes protects the moon and holds it down. It must be the diamond. This is the reason I am here."

"Then how do we get out of here?" Moon Man stood, ignoring Mr. Brown's hand.

"Twelve mighty doors fell," Mr. Brown stepped over to the ten o'clock position, "but only eleven were solid."

There, carved through the oak, was a square hole allowing passage into only one of the hallways.

"And how do we get out once we find the treasure?" Moon Man stepped into the hall.

"It pains me to say that I don't know," Mr. Brown walked around him and started down the tunnel. "In any case, I don't think it will be something you will need to worry about."

"If you think you can threaten me…"

"Not a threat, dear boy," Mr. Brown smiled, "merely a deduction. The treasure itself equals freedom."

As they progressed, the discovered old torches stuck in the wall. Mr. Brown brought out his tin of cigarettes and struck a match on the side. "Blast," he said as the torch failed to light, "Ah, there we are." He continued lighting the other torches with the first as they went on.

"We're going in circles," Moon Man noted the curved walls.

"Just one, I believe," Mr. Brown held the torch out. He turned off his lantern and hung it on his belt. "See there!"

Ahead of them, the tunnel opened into a small circular room. There was no other exit, but at the center, strapped to the floor with large chains, was an old wooden hump back chest. It was about two feet tall and three feet long and a foot and a half deep. It was black, but carved with the same celestial motifs that had adorned the metal box and the stone floor and the moon puzzle. Atop the chest, the lid exhibited a large intricately carved moon. The chains that held it were locked by a big metal padlock in the front.

"The treasure," Moon Man exclaimed.

"Freedom," Mr. Brown replied.

"It's bolted down through the floor," Moon Man knelt and lifted the lock. "I don't suppose we have a clue to this key?"

He turned back around to see Mr. Brown pulling a gun out of his vest holster, "I have everything I need."

Moon Man's mind raced. He raised his flashlight to throw.

"Step aside," Mr. Brown directed. "I need a clear shot at the lock. These old eyes may be duller than in the past, but I can still hit the moon with a proper bullet."

"I'm not so sure I like that analogy," Moon Man stood and lowered his light at the same time. He stepped over to Mr. Brown, shoulder to shoulder, and looked down on him.

"I told you I wasn't finished with you," Mr. Brown aimed. "You don't expect me to carry this parcel out on my own, do you?"

He fired a single shot, and the padlock thrashed violently. The bullet bounced across the room and lodged in the wall. A second shot knocked the cartridge apart and sent parts flying.

"That did it," Mr. Brown took a single step towards the chest and froze.

As the clasp of the lock fell away, the chains snapped like they were on a spring and fell into the floor like they were fleeing snakes. The far wall erupted into the ceiling as the heavy weight below the floor was released from the chains.

"My word!" Mr. Brown holstered his gun.

"Looks like the chains equal freedom," Moon Man commented. "Ironic."

"The chains were holding down the moon!" Mr. Brown fell to his knees in front of the chest. "Chains are indeed the Ultimate Passion of Woes upon mankind!"

Without waiting, Mr. Brown pulled at the lid, and fought against the rusty cast iron hinges. "Open!" he shouted as the lid flew back.

Moon Man turned his light up to full power and shone it down on the treasure.

"What?" Mr. Brown reached in. "No!"

He pulled out a stack of bills. One after another, stack after stack of cash was pulled out. Piles were tied together with thin strands of hemp.

"No!" he cried and buried his face in the papers. "It's money! It's just money!"

"What's wrong with money?" Moon Man picked up a wad.

"Dinjab money!" Mr. Brown flung the bills down. "It's worthless now."

"Hm," Moon Man dropped his own handful of bills. "People died for *this*."

"Worthless people," Mr. Brown snarled. His face took on a dark contour. "The kind that rob and fight and hurt those wretched poor you struggle so vainly to help."

Moon Man bent over and picked up some of the bills. He tossed them back into the chest. "I had to learn, I had to accept that what I did, the theft, was for the greater good. It was still wrong, but it was replaceable, if ill gotten. Money is fluid. It comes and goes. Life is not so transient. The money I take is not my money, and I have no real right or claim to it, but I can excuse it as doing something for the betterment of the masses. There is no excuse for taking a life, save perhaps self defense. Some would argue not even then."

"What price freedom, then?" Mr. Brown stood up and looked down. He wiped his hands on his pants. "Do we not go to war and kill for our own devices?"

"I suppose," Moon Man stood beside Mr. Brown, and joined his gaze into the stash of cash. He reached over and pulled the lid closed. "And once enough blood is shed, and once freedom is attained, this booty may once again be worth something."

"Perhaps," Mr. Brown sighed. "At any rate, I promised the Princess of Dinjab that I would bring her this treasure."

"Fine," Moon Man bent over at the side of the chest and took hold of the ornate handle. "Lead the way."

Mr. Brown grunted as he lifted the chest behind his back.

"Gah!" Moon Man dropped his end and fell to one knee after only moving the chest a couple of feet. He dropped his hands to the floor and pulled at his gloves in a fury, "My God, that's heavy! My hands are on *fire!*"

Mr. Brown lost his grip and fell over into the wall as the chest dropped. "For pity's sake, man!" he cried. "You nearly ripped my arms out of the sockets!"

Moon Man tucked his gloves into his pocket next to his gun, "Yes, well, it's better than having a bullet graze the back of your hand." He held up his swollen bloody hands.

"Yes… well…" Mr. Brown got back in position. "Take your time, then. Just try to warn me next time."

The men struggled down and around a sloping tunnel, stopping to rest and to light the torches along the wall. After a few hundred feet, the tunnel opened up through a recently broken wall.

"Must have happened when the chains fell," Moon Man looked around.

"Undoubtedly," Mr. Brown grunted.

They found themselves in the large square room where Moon Man had fought the Dream Man. Everything was the same, except an old torch burned in a sconce on the wall, and the Dream Man was gone.

"It took slightly longer than I thought," Mr. Brown shuffled past the body of one of Marcetti's thugs, the delusional gentleman must have come around and escaped."

"More than I can say for these poor…"

"Yaaaahh!" the Dream Man leapt down from the alcove above onto the back of the chest.

Moon Man flew backwards, and Mr. Brown stumbled forwards, and fell face first into one of the small channels of water.

Moon Man leapt up, but was back handed by the now chalk faced, wild eyed Dream Man. He was sent spinning and tripped backwards over Marcetti and fell to one knee.

"Mine!" the Dream Man dragged the chest over to the dark exit. "I get it! I get it *all!*"

Klang!

A large shovel swept down out of the darkness and smashed the Dream

Man in the head. He fell down immediately.

"You got it, alright," Angel stepped out of the darkness with the shovel over his shoulder. "What happened here?"

"Imbecile!" a soaking wet Mr. Brown trudged over to the unconscious Dream Man. "You dare to strike *me?*" He pulled out his gun and pointed it at the Dream Man's head.

"Whoa!" Angel dropped his shovel and raised his hands. "Hold on, now."

"No!" Moon Man whipped out his .45 and gritted his teeth.

"Now, Stephen," Mr. Brown continued to hold his gun on the Dream Man. "Your hands are injured and exhausted. I doubt you could even pull the trigger."

"*I* could," Angel cocked his gun against Mr. Brown's temple.

"He will only cause you more trouble," Mr. Brown lowered his gun. A hardness fell over him. "I've learned when to take out my enemies."

"Not your call," Angel reached over and took Mr. Brown's gun from him.

Mr. Brown twitched and spat. "I should have killed him when I shot Marcetti and his misanthropes," he sneered. His accent became thicker as he harshly whispered under his breath, "Had I known the puzzle clue was a lie, I would have just shot you through the heart instead of the helmet before you even entered."

"*You* were the one who shot me?"

"Of course," Mr. Brown said. "I needed the diversion. You know the importance of this crate."

"And you admit it with a gun to your head?" Moon Man lowered his own gun.

"You think I am unprepared?" Mr. Brown looked away. "I always have contingencies. Plus I have the courage of my convictions. You forget who knows your secrets."

"This is the guy?" Angel eyed him. "Say the word, Boss. We can't let him ruin everything."

No," Moon Man held up his hands for Angel to see. "We can't have his blood on our hands. We'll get through this."

"Likely not," Mr. Brown argued. "But I told you I would never use this information against you, and I shan't."

"With all the folks Moon Man's helped," Angel pointed his gun closer. "You'd be the one to suffer more than him."

Moon Man stooped to pick up the chest.

"I'd a' been here sooner, but somebody whacked me in the head from behind," Angel rubbed the back of his head. "I hope it was this crazy guy. Payback feels good."

"Let's get out of here," Moon Man said to Angel. "I'll explain as we go, and then Mr. Brown here is headed to a jail cell."

"I will be needed to deliver the vital…"

"I'll deliver the money to the princess," Moon Man glared behind his helmet. "It's my method of operations, remember?"

"Hold up," Angel handed Mr. Brown's gun to Moon Man, and holstered his own. "Let me get this. Those hands look pretty tender."

"You'll get no argument from me," Moon Man stood and stretched his back.

"Honor would dictate you help your elder," Mr. Brown struggled with the front of the chest.

"You lost your right to speak of honor long ago," Moon Man said.

Moon Man explained the night to Angel as they backtracked to the entrance. When they approached the final spiral staircase, Moon Man saw the motion of lights outside.

"Hold on," he said. "Someone's out there."

"It is my party," Mr. Brown sniffed. "They have tired of waiting. She is not known for her patience."

"She?" Angel said.

"The Princess of Dinjab," Mr. Brown rolled his eyes. "Were you not listening to the explanation so adroitly summarized by Mr. Stephens as we trudged our way back?"

"So, we're just supposed to…" Angel stepped out into the wet sand with the chest. Moon Man nearly walked into him when he stopped short.

A dozen men in dark green military garb with white stripes down the side, pointed rifles at them. The men wore stylized hats and the flag of the old Dinjab empire on their sleeves. Amidst the men, on a silk draped chair being held aloft on a panel by a man in the front and back, was a beautiful young Dinjabi woman in a red gown and a cat mask. Moon Man was surprised that he actually knew her.

"Pussycat?" he stepped around Angel who was setting the chest down.

"Stop!" she put out her hand. Her men all raised their rifles to position.

Moon Man stopped and raised his hands.

"Pussycat is the princess?" Angel also raised his hands. "But she's a known thief."

"Yes," Moon Man said, "who usually works out of Yorktown. Does your boyfriend know you're doing this, Pussycat?"

"The Owl is busy elsewhere tonight," Mr. Brown stepped over to the soldiers. "We saw to that."

"Where's your…" Moon Man began. "Oh…"

A giant of a man stepped out from behind the large river willow on the bank. He was wearing parachute pants and a turban, and instead of a shirt, he had a rippling amount of muscles. He stood behind the soldiers with his arms crossed.

"Lun-Pun, right?" Moon Man looked way up to the giant's face.

"We retrieved the treasure," Mr. Brown told Pussycat.

"Let us see it, then," she spoke with an upper class British accent.

Mr. Brown stood in front of Moon man, "My weapon, if you please."

Moon Man looked over at the Pussycat.

"You live because of my agreement with the Owl," the princess said, "and because my cause is righteous."

Moon Man handed the gun over.

"I have no such agreements," Mr. Brown grabbed his gun, intentionally slapping Moon Man's sore hands. "But tonight we follow the rules of the lady with all the soldiers."

"And the giant manservant," Moon Man reminded.

Mr. Brown opened the chest and moved several stacks of money aside. He popped open a side panel, and pulled out a handful of gold necklaces that sparkled with precious gems in the moonlight. "Did I neglect to inform you of the hidden panels?" he said to Moon Man.

"This man is not to be trusted," Moon Man said to the princess. "He's not the great detective. He'll double cross you!"

"He is being well compensated, and is under my protection," the princess waved her hand, and two soldiers came down and picked up the chest. "I know who he is." She turned to Mr. Brown, "Is the Crescent Moon there?"

"We can search better in the light, away from prying eyes."

"You'll never get away with this," Moon Man threatened. "Evil is always found out."

"I've been getting away with this longer than you have been alive, young man. Have you ever heard the term, arch nemesis?" Mr. Brown tucked his gun away along with one of the necklaces he took from the chest. "It wasn't even a term in the English language before I came along. It was defined by me. I am the original and the best."

The soldiers carried the chest up to the giant, Lun-Pun, who picked up the entire thing with one hand and set it on his shoulder.

"Best for you two to stay here until we're gone," Pussycat suggested. "I wouldn't want any of my men to have to protect me. They are all itching for a fight. Cheerio!"

As the group marched up the hill into the weeds and the darkness, Moon Man fell to his knees.

"Boss!" Angel ran up and put his hand on Moon Man's shoulder.

"Hard fought victory," Moon Man hung his head. "Let's get back to the car."

"Victory?" Angel put Moon Man's arm around his shoulder and lifted him up. He helped him as they stumbled through the undergrowth, "A few more victories like that will put us in our graves."

They finally got to the car and unloaded their gear. Moon Man fell into the back seat, and immediately took off his helmet. "I think I need a doctor," he looked at his hands.

"Yeah. We need to get you to a doctor," Angel opened the front door and got in.

"Then we're agreed, Angel."

"So, Boss, how was this a victory?" Angel started the car.

"That money, or at least the jewels, will help fund an important fight," Stephen Thatcher pulled his gloves out of his pocket and set them beside him in the seat.

"If they don't just keep it," Angel said. "You reckon that Crescent Moon Diamond was in the hidden panels?"

"The value of that stone is worth ten times the value of whatever is in that chest, even if the cash were good," Thatcher loosened his vest. "It's a priceless symbol that'll only be worth more once the revolution gets truly underway."

"I don't trust it in the hands of those two," Angel shook his head. "The Pussycat has never been a freedom fighter, or even very responsible with her goods."

"I don't trust them either," Moon Man took a small square copper box out of his glove, and held it up.

Angel nearly ran off the road. He skidded to a stop along the shoulder, "Boss, is that...?"

Moon Man opened the box to reveal a large perfect diamond. It glowed supernaturally in the soft blue moonlight shining in through the opening in the roof.

"This will do more for the cause than any treasure," Moon Man said. "I found this in a niche beneath the chest. I feigned injury, and tucked it into my glove. It was *below* the treasure chest, Angel."

"Yeah?"

"So, chains weren't holding down the moon. The treasure helped protect it, but the Ultimate Passion of Woes is money and the love of it."

"Well, I'll be," Angel grinned. "So what'll happen when Mr. Brown discovers there's no Moon. What'll we do about him knowing our secret?"

"Well.. heh..."

"What?"

"We'll cross that bridge when we get to it." Stephen Thatcher looked up and rolled his eyes.

"You *are* tired."

"Let's get me home and changed," the detective closed the box and tucked it away.

"Then to the doc?"

"Yeah, but we'll have to come up with a good reason for it."

"Hunting accident?"

"At night?" Thatcher looked out the window. "No, I don't think so. Plus, we've used that one before. Ah, I've got it."

"What?"

"We can say I've been trying to make a few extra bucks. I've taken on a part time job down at the docks, or something."

"Working another job at night?"

"Yeah, you know," Moon Man smiled, "moonlighting."

THE END

MOON MAN- PHASES

I didn't really believe in Robin Hood…

The idea that all rich people were somehow inherently evil and that it was just to steal from them was the twisted logic taken from the original Robin Hood tales, which were originally less about class hatred and vengeance politics and more about the ruthlessness of monarchy and the value of every human life. That's because Robin Hood wasn't written for us. His type, though, spoke to a lot of people stuck in a depression era life, and thus came Moon Man. My opinion started to vary slightly. What use would a Moon Man have to today's readers?

Well, there are those, of course, who agree with the modern Robin Hood type. I could, I suppose, emphasize that all the people he stole from were bad. No, there was something more to the pulp sensibility than that, an adventurous tone that was more prevalent than the moral fables of the Robin Hood mythos. I needed to focus more on the pulp and less on the preach. With that, the way I looked at Stephen Thatcher waxed and waned somewhat more.

His voice, I needed his voice. This was keeping me on the dark side of the story. Editor Ron Fortier and I mulled it over, and he helped shine a little flashlight on who our character was. He was an intelligent man who loved puzzles. He was hunted and hated by the law and the lawless, but he had helpers on both sides, people who believed in him, on his cause. His cause… Just what was it? Was it to punish the guilty like many of his counterparts? No, it was more positive than that. It was just to help the downtrodden, those who the rest of society had abandoned. He helped give some light in their dark times. He couldn't cure their ills. He couldn't eliminate the cause, but he could alleviate some of the symptoms. The money he provided could help, even if just for a while, to get them through the dark nights.

But, where would he get his treasure? How about, quite literally a treasure? I could showcase his personality and his motivation, his friends and enemies in a way that acknowledged but avoided the politics of his actions. I wanted a pulp, not a manifesto. Now, the light was beginning to shine full. Now, the story began to unfold. I still didn't believe in Robin Hood, but the Moon Man was not Robin Hood. I could see that now.

With the clouds out of the way, I was able to send our hero off on a daring quest full of fists and bullets and crazy characters. I hope you find your treasure satisfying.

DAVID NOE - David Noe (No'-ee) is the story editor and cofounder of InDELLible Comics, a new company bringing public domain comic book characters back from the old Dell Comics Group. The first comics should be out right now! He has written several short story collections that are also available on Amazon in paperback or digital (Kin, Voices In My Pen, With A Twist, Welcome To Honeycomb, USA), three poetry collections, and counting (Scanner Code, New Things Among the Old, The Thrill of Drowning), some comic book scripts, a nonfiction book about renting (Living In Someone Else's House), a western (The Alabaster Kid, Beneath the Veil) and a couple of other pulp stories (The Purple Scar volume 2, Slipknot and the Golden Claw). He also has a series of speculative urban fantasy type books called, The Trade of the Tricks (The Tricks' Brand and Saga, Book 1).

He likes mixing humor with his action.

FROM DUSK TILL DAWN
By J. L. LaMastus

It was a dreary night. And the apartment building was dark with the exception of one lit room. The only room that was occupied. Though it was now emptying out.

"Sorry Detective, not today." The man in the moon shaped helmet laughed as he stood on the fire escape just beyond the reach of the frustrated Lieutenant Detective. It seemed that once more the Moon Man was going to elude his grasp. Gil McEwen snarled and swore as he watched his prey slide down the ladder and dash off into the streets of Great City. It was just unacceptable.

"One of these days." He muttered at the figure shrinking in the distance. Yes, one of these days he would finally apprehend the Moon Man and unmask him. Ending once and for all the game of cat and mouse that they had been so long engaged in. But today was not to be that day.

For his part the Moon Man himself was quite relieved about that. He mused about it briefly before turning his thoughts elsewhere. There were other things he needed to worry about. He had plans for later this evening after all. Important plans that he had admittedly put at risk with this little adventure. But it felt like there hadn't been much of a choice in the matter for him. He had learned that the notorious "Big Tommy" would be leaving town tonight and he needed to get to him before he got away.

The man was a glorified thug and a goon really. And even though he was new in town and was merely just passing through, he'd already made all the right connections during his short visit. Worming his way into the corrupt circles that the Moon Man and the police both fought to bring down. The connections had turned out to be quite lucrative for Big Tommy. If he hadn't been stopped he'd have left town with a whole lot of money that he had no right to. That wouldn't be happening now however.

Before the good Lieutenant Detective Gil McEwen had arrived the Moon Man had confronted the thug and had a little "conversation" with him. It hadn't gone as well as he'd hoped however. Moon Man rubbed his ribs gingerly. Those were going to be smarting for a while. Still he'd gotten the best of his opponent, and started to make off with the money. He was just finishing up when McEwen came bursting in on them. Moon Man had leapt out the window as the Detective had stumbled over Big Tommy's prone form. It was almost comical to see as he glanced back in the window. The sight alone had almost made the sore ribs worth it.

He thought about the money he now carried in a satchel over his shoulder. He'd pass it along to "Angel" in the morning. Knowing that his ally could be trusted to see that it was put to good use. Helping the poor citizens of Great City in their need. As always it wasn't enough, but every little bit helped. That was for tomorrow though. Tonight he was Moon Man no more.

Tonight he was just Stephen Thatcher for the rest of the evening. And Mr. Stephen Thatcher had a date with his fiancé that he needed to get to.

It sure was a fine evening for a night out. Or so Stephen Thatcher thought at least. That was why he had decided to take his fiancé Sue McEwen to the Northern Pioneer tonight. A nice new place that had recently opened up and she'd been anxious to try it. It was also to be a much needed break from their hectic life of late. They were enjoying a fine steak dinner and discussing wedding plans. Well, Sue was discussing anyway, Stephen was doing his best to pay attention though. Sue was full to overflowing with ideas that she wanted to share with him. He listened but his mind kept wanting to wander off.

Not surprising as Stephen had a lot going on of late. And even though Sue knew about it, he was actually the mysterious Moon Man. To some a benefactor, to criminals a threat and to the police which included both his and Sue's fathers, he was a dangerous criminal himself who needed to be brought to justice. But Sue was the only one who knew the truth of his actions as Moon Man. That he was secretly working for the good of the people of their city. For what he stole was only from the corrupt and dishonest. And not for his personal gain either. No, it was that there were so many poor and desperate people in Great City who had no one to help them. No one except the Moon Man that was. All he took he gave to them with the aid of his one ally. A man named Ned "Angel" Dargen. Ned was the one who found the people who needed the help most and he distributed the money to them for Moon Man. But tonight was not supposed to be a night for any of that. Stephen had promised this evening to Sue. While he had sworn to help the poor and it was hard for him not to think about that, she needed his attention too. And he was determined to give it to her tonight.

"So you're okay with that?" Sue asked, looking at him from across the table. She smiled warmly as she waited for his response. "Yes, I think it's wonderful. We'll do it."

"Oh, good. I was afraid you wouldn't go for it."

He returned her smile and assured her he meant it. Then he looked across the room when he heard the commotion. Stephen spied a situation at one of the other dinner's tables. A rough looking young man had grabbed his waiter and was shaking him rather violently. There was no need for that sort of behavior and Stephen Thatcher wasn't about to sit there and let it happen. "Excuse me dear." He said as he took to his feet and made his way across the room. Sue watched as he confronted the man who was accosting the poor waiter. She saw the glint of light on metal as her fiancé showed his badge. Sue couldn't hear what was being said but she was sure Stephen was giving him a good scolding. Good for him she thought. She was proud to see her future husband in action as himself rather than as the Moon Man. Shortly the man was seated back in his chair and appeared to be apologizing profusely. Oh good, she thought, it seemed the situation was resolved. And a moment later Stephen was rejoining her. "What was that all about?"

"Oh it was nothing really. The rough gentleman was mistaken that was all. All straightened up now." He told her and she let the matter drop. No sense in letting it spoil their dinner after all.

They resumed their meal along with the discussion of the plans for their wedding. Sue continued with her list of ideas. Most of which he was fine with, though there were a couple he had to shoot down. Much too grandiose for a policeman's wedding after all. Stephen's mind began to drift once more; lulled by the good food and the music the band was playing. Slowly Sue McEwen was losing his attention. "Dear. Is everything okay?" Oh no, she had noticed his distraction.

"Oh, yes. I'm sorry my dear." He got a sheepish look on his face. "I should be paying you more attention shouldn't I?"

"Yes you should. But this has something to do with work, doesn't it?"

"No not really."

"Says you. I know you and father have been hard at work on some new case all of the past week." Her expression turned quite serious. "And it isn't father's obsession with the Moon Man again. I know that much."

"What? Oh no, the case we've been dealing with actually has nothing to do with that this time. Surprisingly." And that was the truth. Over the past couple of weeks a new crime wave seemed to have started. Three masked men in aviator uniforms had been committing a series of daring daylight robberies. Little had been learned about them so far. The leader dressed in a black uniform and his henchmen were clad in white uniforms trimmed in grey. They had been committing some rather audacious robberies, even in the most unusual of places. So far they had hit a grocer's market, a gentleman's club, a gym and even an automat. There seemed to be no rhyme or reason to their choices. And they never really seemed to get away with much either. They had been enough that it had even taken Lieutenant Detective Gil McEwen's mind off of the Moon Man for the time being. Well, except for earlier that evening of course. But that just showed how serious the situation was becoming. It was true that so far no one had been hurt or killed even though the men were armed. But still someone could be eventually. And the amounts they stole had started out small; they were getting larger with each robbery. The police so far had come up empty of any leads or clues. Stephen had decided that the Moon Man might need to look into it as well. So he'd had Angel doing a little asking around on the side to see if he could learn anything that the police couldn't. But so far he had turned up nothing.

"The case does have us stumped dear. But your father is a great detective and you know he always gets his man." Stephen tried to repress a smirk. "Give him time he'll puzzle it all out."

Sue McEwen sighed. "You're right. Then he can get back to hunting the Moon Man again I guess."

"Yes, I suppose he will. But tonight is not supposed to be about discussing cases, Moon Men or mystery airmen robbers. This is our night. Let's enjoy it shall we?" His fiancé gave him the biggest of smiles as she agreed.

With that settled Stephen did better at keeping his mind on topic as they continued to discuss the plans for their wedding. Eventually Sue ran out of her list of ideas and instead she changed the subject to some gossip and current events in Great City. With fortuitous timing the waiter brought out their desserts. Stephen wouldn't have to talk gossip for long. It was something that he was much less interested in discussing.

The pies looked delicious and they picked up their forks to take their first bites. However they were not to enjoy the desserts nor the gossip as a loud crash came from the kitchen; followed by a gunshot and screams. Stephen jumped to his feet and turned to face the kitchen doors ready to see what was going on. He didn't have to wait to find out. Three men stepped through the doors and into the dinning room.

Stephen and Sue looked on in shock. It was the very men they had just been discussing. The three of them were dressed in aviator's uniforms lacking any insignia or markings. The one in front, obviously their leader wore all black head to toe. The two behind him wore white outfits trimmed with some grey. Their faces covered in masks and goggles. Each of them held a gun in hand as they surveyed the room. Everyone sat frozen in their seats with fear. Only Stephen was still on his feet. Though unarmed there wasn't much he could do at the moment.

"Okay ladies and gentlemen I'm certain you know the routine." The man in black addressed the dinners. "Do as we ask and this will all be over quickly and no one has to come to any harm."

Stephen slowly returned to his seat. For now it seemed best to go along with the robbers. At least until an opportunity to act came up. So he watched as the black clad leader directed his minions to do their dirty work. One by one they visited the tables and relieved the patrons of their valuables. Working their way through the room the two men came to the table where the young man who'd caused the disturbance sat. Stephen noticed that they spent a little more time at his table than any of the others. That was odd, he thought. But he didn't have time to dwell on it.

At last they came to the table where he and his fiancé, Sue were seated. She glared at them as Stephen Thatcher handed over his wallet and her necklace and bracelet.

"Dusk." The taller thinner of the two called out to their leader. So that was his name. "We've got an officer of the law here."

"Keep an eye on him." Dusk strode over to the table. He looked down on them through his dark tinted goggles. "Remember officer; don't be tempted to try anything heroic. I really don't want anyone harmed. So far we haven't hurt anyone as you know. And I'd really like to keep it that way." Well, that was rather noble of him. Of course he was still robbing them. Stephen decided to wait and see how this played out. He didn't want anyone here coming to harm either after all.

"I won't try anything. I'm not packing and I don't want anyone to get hurt either." Stephen assured him. Dusk nodded at him. "Good man." Then turning to his associates, "Dawn. Let's finish this up and be on our way." So, Dusk and Dawn. Well now at least he knew what they called themselves. Clever names Stephen supposed. But what was with the aviator uniforms? Maybe they made their getaway in planes? No. If they did that the police would already know about it. Maybe they were pilots however. There was no time for speculation at the moment. They were finishing up and preparing to leave.

Stephen placed his hand on Sue's. "I'm going to see if I can follow them." He whispered. "Let your father know when he gets here." Sue nodded. They both knew that when word got to headquarters Gil McEwen would be the first one on the scene.

"Ladies, gentlemen." Dusk called for attention. "We thank you for your generous cooperation. We have enjoyed your company, be we really must be going now." He looked directly at Thatcher and with a nod he walked out followed by Dawn. Stephen Thatcher waited a few moments then he got up and followed them at a discrete distance.

Outside the Northern Pioneer he saw them climb into a beat up older car and proceed to drive off. It made quite a racket as they attempted to speed away. Well, they should be easy to follow in that Stephen thought. There was no time to change into his Moon Man garb though, as he needed to get after them. He got into his own car and drove off in pursuit.

"Are you okay?" Gil McEwen asked his daughter as his men interviewed the other restaurant patrons. She told him she was fine and filled him in on the details of what had happened. Finally ending with telling him that her fiancé was on their tail as they spoke.

"Excellent. He'll track 'em down and we can finally bring them to justice." Gil didn't even try to suppress a grin. After weeks of nothing they finally had a break. "So. They called themselves Dusk and Dawn. Well that's something new." He wasn't too sure what to make of their names. Though it made some sort of sense what with the black and white outfits. But still, "What is it with masked weirdos in this town?"

Gil McEwen compared notes with his men. It was pretty much the same story. It struck him as odd that even though they were armed Dusk and Dawn wanted to ensure that no one was hurt. Just as in their previous robberies. Whatever their motivation he was glad they weren't harming anyone or killing. But they were still stealing and they had to be caught. Sooner or later someone would get hurt. And that was something the lieutenant detective wanted to avoid.

With Stephen Thatcher on their tail he was confident that they would be caught. Quite possibly even before this night was over. We had better be ready he thought. As soon as Thatcher gets word to us we'll need to be prepared. McEwen went over with his men working up a plan for when they heard from Sergeant Detective Thatcher. They finished up questioning the witnesses then made their way back to headquarters to get ready.

Driving through the streets of Great City Stephen Thatcher was wishing he could call in and report. Or get in contact with Angel at least. So far he was sure that the culprits were leading him on a merry goose chase. Perhaps they had spotted him and were giving him a run around in hopes of losing their pursuer. He had to stick with them though. He needed to find their hideout.

They led him down a few of the same streets again. They weren't going in circles exactly however. They were slowly making progress across town. Gradually heading to the west side of the city. He got the feeling that this seemed like they planned it in case they were followed. If so then perhaps they didn't know he was after them. And the Moon Man would still have the advantage of surprise.

He read the sign that said Charlie the Butchers again. Well this was the third time they had passed his shop. And they hadn't stopped for steaks yet. Not the time for jokes Thatcher thought to himself. He had to focus on the job at hand. Keeping up the tail and finding out where they were going.

Finally they stopped repeating their route and were headed in a distinctly different direction. They turned off on a side street and were soon on an underused road that led to the outskirts of Great City. Thatcher hadn't been through this way in a long time. A couple of years or more at least. He racked his brain trying to remember just what was out here. It was mostly undeveloped fields and some farms if he remembered correctly. And then it hit him, what was out here. The old airfield! It made perfect sense. That had to be where they were headed.

"So I guess they are pilots after all."

It seemed very likely that they could have a plane waiting for them at the airfield. A great get away vehicle. And if so he would have to do something to stop them before they could take off. He didn't have time to stop and call headquarters. And even if he did, out here there was nowhere for him to call from. He couldn't turn back, as the airfield may not be where they were headed. So he was on his own. More accurately Moon Man was on his own.

Unfortunately there were no shortcuts he could take to beat them to the airfield. This road was the only one. He would have to follow them until they arrived and hope to prevent their escape.

Dusk and Dawn had removed their masks and were focused on where they were going. If anyone had been following them the crazy route they had taken through the city streets should have lost them. So they were starting to relax some. "Good thing that flatfoot decided to play nice." The heavy set Dawn said. "I'd have hated it if we'd had our hand forced." As he turned the car onto the long stretch of road leading to the field. The taller skinny Dawn nodded his agreement. "Yeah. We were lucky that time."

Dusk sat in the backseat alone looking contemplative. So far their luck had been holding out. He'd been telling the truth when he said he didn't want anyone hurt by their actions. Neither did his two partners. They needed the money of course, but they weren't cold blooded killers after all. Not anymore at least. Not since the War. And that was different, the Heinie were the enemy and they had it coming.

But the War was over and now they had found themselves grounded. "I don't like it either men. But this is our mission now." He looked off in front of them. Their wings had been taken away from them. And though they'd been heroes not so long ago they now found that no one wanted them anymore.

"So I guess they are pilots after all."

Well almost no one. "Mark, did you make the exchange?"

"Yes sir." Heavy Dawn replied. "The contact has the papers and no one's the wiser."

"I really don't like us playing spies sir." Tall Dawn added in. "And this whole robbery cover rubs me wrong."

"Duly noted Larry." Dusk couldn't fault his men. They were good soldiers and were following orders just like he was. "This should be the last assignment for us."

"But sir, what if it isn't?" Dawn Larry asked. "We're in pretty deep now. I know you're our C.O. but who's really been giving us these orders? And can we trust them to let us quit?"

Dusk didn't have a good answer for that one. They'd been contacted a month back by a man they didn't know. He claimed to be a government agent and he seemed to have legitimate credentials and most importantly he had a mission for them. They'd been grounded, had their wings clipped and had fallen onto hard times. Mark had been hitting the bottle pretty heavy. As for Larry, he didn't want to think about that. It had been a struggle and they were getting desperate. He hadn't questioned it, just accepted the assignment. They had been making hand offs of some documents at each of their "robberies." And though it made him uncomfortable they'd been ordered to keep the money they got from the jobs. They needed it, times were hard and they weren't the heroes people had loved just a few years before. During the war the three of them had flown countless missions and done many heroic acts. Now they were reduced to common criminals. Or so it seemed. He wasn't sure that it was nothing more than a cover for the important mission of getting the documents into the hands of other agents.

But this was supposed to be the last one. They had saved some of the money they had acquired and he had a plan. They were using it to buy the airfield that had been shut down and were fixing it up.

"We'll be back in the air soon enough boys."

"You think we got enough tonight Sir?" Dawn Mark asked. "To get our planes back up and running?"

"Not quite. But it will be enough to give us a good start."

"See, I told ya we'd be getting our wings back. They couldn't keep 'em away from us." Dawn Larry added. "You need to have faith in our C.O."

"Yeah yeah." Dawn Mark looked up the road ahead. "Anyway we're almost there Sir."

"Excellent. You men did a great job tonight. And once more, no one was harmed. I'm proud of the both of you."

Back at the airfield they could report in and be done with all this spy stuff.

After tonight they could get the planes back up and get their air delivery business off the ground so to speak. And do honest work once more.

Stephen Thatcher, the Moon Man wasn't feeling too proud. He had been pursuing Dusk and Dawn since they got away from the restaurant and he still wasn't sure what he was going to be able to do once he caught up with them. The old airfield had been shut down for several years and there would be no way he could call for backup. But he couldn't turn back to make the call. Not if they had a plane waiting for them. They'd be long gone before he or the backup would arrive. "It'll be up to the Moon Man to stop them." But that would require taking the time to change. Would he have that time though? Hopefully he would.

He would find out soon as they were drawing nearer to the airfield. The field was dark he noted. A good sign that there wasn't a plane ready and waiting for them. If they were leaving they wouldn't be taking off anytime soon. They'd need to turn on the lights and get a plane going. That would take time to do. Time he could use to stop them after all.

He watched as they parked next to one of the buildings and went in. The lights turned on in the small shack. It wasn't a hangar, more likely the airfield offices. This had to be their hideout. Of course, they were dressed like pilots so why wouldn't they be working out of an abandoned airfield? Stephen had stopped his car not daring to go any closer. He didn't want to be heard driving up and lose the element of surprise. At least now he would have time to change into Moon Man before confronting them.

He opened up the trunk and pulled out a case. Opening it he removed a black robe and gloves and donned them. Then he took out the spherical argus glass helmet and placed it over his head. With the rebreather he would be able to see out and not have to worry about Dusk and his henchmen being able to see him. Next he took out his gun, hoping it wouldn't come to that but he knew that it could become necessary to deal with them.

"Well I'm ready." He stood up straight and started walking towards the building.

Inside Dusk was on the phone. "Yes the hand-off was made. We're ready to end this assignment." He told the person on the other end of the line. And they were ready to end it. Dusk and his men had enough of these assignments, playing robbers to deliver the paperwork. There should have been a better cover, but they were desperate and so they went along with it. But this had been promised to be the last time. "They're on their way. This is finally done."

Dawn Mark peered out the window. "Sir. There's someone out there. I saw headlights down the road then they disappeared. It's too dark to tell but I think I see someone moving out there."

"Masks men. Leave the lights on. We don't want to give away that we know we have a visitor." The two men put their masks and goggles back on and drew out their pistols. For his part Dusk held off on drawing his. "It could be the detective from the restaurant. Perhaps he decided since he couldn't do anything there he would follow us and see where we went."

"He may be out there then?"

"Maybe. Or maybe not. He might have gone back to get back-up. Now that he knows where we are."

"But I thought I saw someone moving out there. And what if it isn't the detective?"

"We shall just have to see. Be ready. We need to deal with this before they get here."

The Dawn took up positions on either side of the door. It wasn't the only entrance; however it was the most likely one. Dusk glanced behind him at the other door. Bolted and rusted shut as it hadn't been used since the air field had been shut down. If anyone tried to use that door they'd know it. That left the two windows on his left, the one on his right and the sky light. Would they be able to hear someone climbing to the roof? Very probably, so they should be safe from that direction. Yes the front door was really the most likely way in.

Moon Man was thinking the very same thing. He prowled around the building as noiselessly as possible. Seeing the rust and corrosion on the backdoor he didn't want to try it. There seemed to be no access to the roof. The windows were a possibility but he would have to smash his way in. Of course he couldn't just open the front door and stroll on in either.

Moon Man dared a glance through the nearest window. He saw the two Dawns stationed on either side of the door. Guns drawn and at the ready. "So, they're expecting me." He thought, wary now. I could wait them out, I suppose. Eventually they have to get tired of standing there expecting someone to come in.

"You had something for me Owens?" McEwen paced behind his desk. He had been getting anxious waiting to hear from Thatcher. This new patrolman,

Owens thought he might have something. So Gil wanted to hear what he had to say.

"Well Sir." Owens handed him a flyer. "I thought this might be important."

The flier was for a new business. The Dusk Till Dawn Air Delivery Service. They were to be staring up in a couple of weeks and were operating out of the old airfield that had been shut down a while back.

"We know the robbers have been dressed in aviator uniforms and now we know they go by the names Dusk and Dawn. Seems like a bit more than a coincidence that this outfit is starting up now."

"Seems a bit too obvious to me." Gil was skeptical. "But still it would be worth looking into. Get a couple of the guys to go with you and see if anything's up at this airfield."

"Yes Sir." Owens turned and left the office. He grabbed the other patrolmen and they headed out to the airfield. With luck his hunch would turn out to be right.

Dusk was growing restless. He paced the room while the Dawns stood guard at the door. "This is pointless." He announced at last. "Surely our guest has had time to get here and make themselves known."

He crossed the room and started to unmask. But then something held him back. Leaving the mask in place he instructed one of his men to go outside and patrol the perimeter while the other remained on guard with him inside.

Dawn Mark softly opened the door and took a step outside. Looking around to the left and to the right he saw nothing. And so closed the door and made a counter clockwise path around the building.

Behind some nearby shrubs Moon Man observed as the heavier Dawn was making his rounds of the building. This was the opportunity he was waiting for. Abandoning his post he prowled around behind Dawn Mark, sneaking up on him. With a swift blow to the head Dawn Mark slumped to the ground unconscious. He'll be out like a light for a little while, Moon Man figured. That just leaves the two inside. Better odds now.

Moon Man looked around as he drew near the door. Not sure what he was searching for he glanced around. Maybe there would be something that he could use to his advantage. But he could find nothing and so he just kicked the door in and rushed through. A gun went off as he jumped to his feet and dodged the bullet. Moon Man knew he had to make this quick. But Dawn Larry was already on him, tackling him to the floor.

"Moon Man! What is he doing here?"

Dusk holstered his gun and attempted to join the fray, even though it seemed unnecessary. Dawn Larry had things well in hand and he could do little but get in his man's way. Dawn got Moon Man in a choke hold and had him down to one knee. But Moon Man turned the tables on him and flipped Dawn over his shoulders. He checked his helmet quickly to make sure it was still secure. Then he looked down on his opponent. Dawn was slowly rising to his feet. He couldn't be given that chance however. Moon Man kicked him in the knee and he dropped to the floor once more. With a swift boot to the head the foe was unconscious. That just left the leader, Dusk to deal with.

Moon Man turned to face his remaining opponent. "It's just you now. Both of your men are out."

"Let's not waste time on words Moon Man. I don't care why you're here. I'll finish you off and that will be the end for you."

With those words Dusk took a swing at Moon Man's argus glass helmet. Moon Man was able to avoid the blow. Knowing that his helmet could have been broken by just that one blow. Not only would it have revealed his identity but the glass could have left him seriously injured. It was best to not let his foe get in a blow like that. He tried to kick Dusk's feet out from under him but Dusk seemed to be expecting the move and easily jumped out of the way.

He didn't have time to recover though as Moon Man made a tackle on him. They both went tumbling to the floor. Moon Man was jarred and glancing to his left he was alarmed. The helmet had a small crack. No, this couldn't happen. He needed to be more careful. He got to his feet and kicked at Dusk once again, but missed. Dusk had rolled out of the way and was now back on his feet as well. Taking a fighting stance Dusk prepared to make his move. Moon Man had let himself get distracted by the damage to his helmet and now he would pay for that mistake.

It was Dusk's turn to attempt a tackle. But he was blocked as Moon Man was able to hold his ground. A hard elbow to the back of the head dazed Dusk and dislodged his hat. Moon Man grabbed Dusk's goggles and twisted them to the side blinding him. This was the opening he needed. If he could just take advantage of it. Dusk attempted to straighten his goggles so that he could see once more. He got them back on right just in time to see the fist flying at his face. He had no time to react and was knocked to the floor and out cold.

Moon Man stood over his fallen opponent and grimaced behind his spherical helmet. With Dusk and Dawn taken out he could relax somewhat. He looked around and found some rope. He proceeded to tie the two of them up and then went outside to get the other Dawn and bring him in to bind with his two compatriots.

But he wasn't there. He must have come to during the fighting. Just then he heard the car engine. Moon Man looked and saw the car speeding off down the road. Blast, he was getting away. "Well I got two of them at least." He said regretfully. "And recovered what they stole I hope." He went back in and unmasked his fallen foes.

He recognized them. That was for sure. But he couldn't seem to place where he'd seen the two men. Just then Dusk began to stir. Maybe he could get some answers from him.

"So, I have some questions."

"I'm sure you do. And they'll be answered soon enough." Dusk replied bruskly. "Where's my other man?"

"He ran off. So much for loyalty."

"Ha. He'll be back."

"Anyway." Moon Man wanted to waste no more time. "Would you care to tell me just what you have been up to?"

"As I said, you'll get answers soon enough Moon Man."

"Sir." Now Dawn was coming to as well. "This man is a criminal."

"You're correct Larry. But not to worry, shortly he'll be dealt with."

"What are you talking about?" But before Moon Man could get the answer they heard a car pulling up. "I guess your henchman decided to come back after all."

"Perhaps."

"Perhaps?" Sue was getting impatient with her father. "You mean you don't know anything yet?"

"No, Steven hasn't reported in." Gil McEwen reassured her. "But I have one of my men checking on a very good lead at this moment."

Sue paced across the room, worried for her fiancé. He had taken off after those robbers Dusk and Dawn hours ago and no one had heard from him since. She knew he could handle himself. Either as Sergeant Detective Stephen Thatcher or as his alter ego The Moon Man. But still it had been some time without any word and she was starting to get worried nonetheless.

Unknown to her she had good reason to be worried. For back at the airfield the car that had pulled up was not the one that Dawn had driven off in. From this car three men stepped out. One tall and heavy set, accompanied by two tough looking bodyguards. They were here to conduct some business with Dusk and Dawn. And they weren't going to be too pleased to find them being held by Moon Man.

"This man is a criminal."

Moon Man turned towards the door, but before he could make another move it swung open. The three men walked in on them. "Don't make any moves you."

Moon Man remained very still as he began working out how he was going to handle this situation. "Well, it looks like we have a situation here." The tall man motioned for his bodyguards to flank Moon Man and his prisoners. "But really this makes it a little easier for us." He explained. "Moon Man came here looking to eliminate his criminal rivals. Which he succeeded in doing. Unfortunately he was mortally wounded himself and was unable to get out before expiring."

"What?" Dusk came to his feet in anger, despite being securely tied up. "You planned to off us all along." Dawn Larry joined him in standing. They faced their traitorous employer with matching glares.

"Oh don't get so worked up. You did a good job for us. But really we can't have any loose ends."

"Moon Man listen." Dusk turned to his captor. "We can straighten this out. Help us and we'll come up with something. You're dead otherwise."

Though it bothered him Moon Man saw the logic in Dusk's argument. He also saw that the Dawn who had fled had returned and was sneaking up behind them through the open door. In his hand he held a length of board ready to strike.

"You're right Dusk. We're in this together for now."

There was a loud crack and the tall man slumped to the floor. His bodyguards spun on their boss' assailant. While they were distracted Moon Man freed Dusk and Dawn Larry. They rushed the bodyguards, but weren't fast enough. Gunshots rang out and Dawn Mark fell back through the door. His white uniform stained crimson he crumpled to the ground. Then they turned to face the new threat of Moon Man, Dusk and the remaining Dawn.

Moon Man ducked low to avoid the bullets. He swerved aside and found himself taking cover behind a table that he overturned. He returned fire on them as he watched to see what Dusk and Dawn would do.

Dusk tackled one of the bodyguards and disarmed him with ease. He then smashed the man's face with the handle of the gun, crushing his nose and taking him out of the fight. That was all he managed before a bullet winged him in the shoulder. The hit was enough to knock him off balance and sent him sprawling. Dawn came to his aid though, drawing the bodyguard's fire.

Dawn got too close for gunplay and he and the bodyguard locked in a struggle. They were pretty evenly matched and neither seemed able to get an upper hand. Dusk and Moon Man could do little but watch on as they secured the other two men.

At last Dawn got the opening he needed. A punch to the gut staggered his foe. He followed up with a strong roundhouse right hand that took the man off his feet. Dawn stood over his fallen foe and looked down on him. "That takes care of that."

The three victors now faced one another. Not sure who would make the next move. Or even what that move might be.

"Well. I guess I should have known he couldn't be trusted." Dusk shook his head. "But I'm a good soldier and he was my C.O. after all."

"Care to fill me in?" Moon Man cocked his head and lowered his weapon. "Explain what's going on and then I'll decide what next."

Dusk let out a sigh. "Very well."

"Sir. Is that a good idea?"

"He's already seen our faces and, well he did help us out. We owe him that at least." So Dusk began his story.

Dusk and his men had been aces in the war. They had come home to the expected hero's welcome. But after a time people moved on, they had been forgotten and things had started to get rough. For proud soldiers like them it had been a struggle. Then one day this government agent approached with a job offer. One they felt they couldn't refuse. An assignment to deliver documents to another agent under the guise of robberies. It seemed odd and Dusk hadn't been entirely comfortable with the idea of it. But no one had stuck up for them and their wings had been taken away. They were grounded and being pushed into the ground it felt like. So he and his men had taken the job.

So for the past few weeks whenever they committed a robbery they had handed off an envelope containing documents of some kind to a man. As Dusk described him Moon Man recognized who he was talking about. Back at the restaurant, the man who had caused the scene arguing with the waiter. The one he'd confronted as Stephen Thatcher.

"I don't know what kind of documents we were handing off." Duck told him. "They were sealed and I obeyed orders. Never looked at them. But now I wonder what they were."

He would have gone on but they heard a car coming down the road. "Listen, I know your reputation. This doesn't involve you. You need to get out of here Moon Man. Let us turn ourselves in." Dusk told him. "We need to face up to what we've done. And we'll have a chance to bring this chump to justice as well. Make things right."

Moon Man mulled it over. It seemed like Dusk was being straight with him. "Fine." He turned and fled the building leaving Dusk and Dawn to deal with whatever came next. As he went he saw the car coming up the road. As it was nearing daybreak he could make out that it was a police cruiser. He wasn't sure how they had found out to come here but he couldn't be seen as Moon Man here.

Patrolman Owens could see the lights on in the building up ahead. Perhaps there was something to his theory after all. Then he saw Stephen's car as they drew closer. He was right and he had to radio it in. They needed to know back at headquarters. Owens pulled to a stop and got on the radio, but while doing so he missed seeing the dark figure dart to the back of Stephen Thatcher's car. If he had he'd have seen the Moon Man disrobing and putting his helmet and other gear in the back of the car. And he would have seen Sergeant Detective Thatcher stepping out from behind the car and heading over towards the nearest hangar. But he was not looking as he gave his report over the radio.

Having reported in, Owens got out and accompanied by the other two patrolmen made his way to the building. Backup was on the way, but Thatcher might be in trouble. They drew closer to the building and could hear men inside talking. Owens dared a glance in the window. He saw unmasked Dusk and one of the Dawns tying up three men. There seemed to be no sign of Thatcher however. Well this was enough for him. He led the other two officers to the door which hung slightly ajar.

They burst in on Dusk and Dawn. Dusk just sighed and raised his hands. "It's okay officers. We're giving ourselves up. And turning in these three for you as well."

Owens was a bit confused, but he accepted it. They handcuffed the robbers, though were unsure what to do about the other men. They only had the word of these criminals about them to go on.

Owens looked around the room and saw the body of the other Dawn on the floor not moving. But there was no sign of Sergeant Detective Thatcher anywhere. "Keep an eye on 'em. I'm going to check around outside."

Owens left and went to look around the building. He found nothing however and started to go back in. About that time he heard cars approaching. Looked like backup was arriving. McEwen was on the ball tonight. Well this morning now actually he realized. He could see the sun rising behind the patrol cars in the distance. They would be here momentarily. That was a relief; however they still needed to find Thatcher.

McEwen questioned Dusk as soon as he got there. He was surprised to hear that Moon Man had shown up. And concerned, as they had yet to find Thatcher. Dusk knew nothing about the missing detective. Or so he claimed at least. McEwen wasn't too sure about the man's story. And these other fellahs they had tied up, that was a head scratcher. They hadn't come to as yet so he wasn't sure what to do with them.

Before he came to a decision he was interrupted. Detective Stephen Thatcher walked in the door rubbing his head. "What the blazes happened to you?"

"I followed these guys here and was sneaking up on the building when I saw someone duck into the hanger. So I decided to check that out." He explained. "Didn't want anyone surprising me. Fat lot of good that did me."

"What do you mean?"

"Someone must have got the jump on me after all. I got conked on the head and the next thing I know I came out of the hangar and saw all of you here."

"Hm." McEwen rubbed his chin. "Was it one of these guys you think?"

"I don't think so. Dusk and his two Dawn were here in the building."

"These other guys?"

"Never saw them. They weren't here as far as I know."

"Well, that leaves the Moon Man then."

"He was here?"

"Yep, you missed out on him. Apparently he's mixed up in this somehow."

Thatcher shook his head. At least his story seemed to convince McEwen. However he didn't notice Owens looking at him with eyes narrowed. Owens had pulled a band of silver paper out of his pocket and was rubbing it between his fingers.

That mystery was solved and McEwen went back to questioning Dusk. He told the Detective about how he and his men had been hired and the documents they had been delivering. When he got to describing the man who had received the hand-offs Thatcher started. He recognized the man as the one who had caused the scene at the restaurant before the robbery. He knew they would have to be looking for him. But perhaps the Moon Man should be the one to find him first.

"Well," McEwen began. "That about wraps that up. Though I need to know why that Moon Man was here. What is his stake in all of this?"

"I can't answer that. He took off after we took care of these guys."

McEwen scratched his chin thoughtfully. There wasn't anything else here. So they gathered them up and headed back to the station.

While the police started their investigation, Moon Man had already begun his own. The next day found the Moon Man talking with "Angel." He explained some of the previous night's events. Enough for him to understand. He then gave the description of the man they were looking for.

"Find out whatever you can about him."

"Yes Boss." Angel would be able to question people on the streets and with luck he would turn up some info on the man before the police did. Three good men had their reputations ruined and one had lost his life because of working with this man and his partners. Moon Man had decided to do what he could to make things right.

That day and the next Angel made the rounds asking questions and trying to find out anything he could. For the most part his inquiries yielded no results. He was beginning to get discouraged and was ready to give it up for the day. But then he got a break.

The man they'd been looking for was a regular at a new night club that had opened just a couple months back. The place already had developed a reputation as being somewhere that the less than savory sort liked to congregate. Angel figured his boss would be interested in that. He knew Moon Man was planning on paying the place a visit here soon anyway. Now he could kill two birds with one stone. Best get back and report what he'd learned.

"Thank you for finding this out for me Angel." Moon Man stood back in the shadows of their meeting place. Pondering his next move.

"Boss. Are you going to check this night club place out?"

"I suppose I shall. It was my plan before the stuff with Dusk and Dawn anyway. Now I just have more reasons to do so."

"Just be careful. I've been hearing some pretty bad stuff about that place."

"Not to worry Angel. I'll be cautious." He dismissed Angel and now being alone removed the helmet of argus glass that hid his identity. He sat at a table and thought about how to best go about things from there. He couldn't just bust into the place. He would have to observe it at first and see what he could learn. But he couldn't take too long. His fellows on the force would be looking out for this contact of Dusk's as well. He could wait and let them handle it sure. But Moon Man had taken this a bit more personally. He wanted to know what was going on and why someone would set up these war heroes the way they had.

And so Stephen Thatcher found himself the next night standing out in front of the club waiting to get in. He was disguised just in case the man he was looking for was here. After their previous run in he was sure to be recognized. And being pointed out as a cop in a place like this could be a hazard to his well being.

He was able to get in without much difficulty and soon found himself seated at a booth in a dark corner of the club. He looked around as he ate the meal he'd ordered. The food was actually quite good and he wished that this could have been a place where he could go to eat.

But Stephen wasn't here for the food he needed to keep his mind on business. He surveyed the room in hopes of seeing the man he was looking for. All the while hoping he didn't catch any undue attention to himself. It was starting to look like this might be a bust. He hadn't seen any sign of the man. Stephen was about to call it a night. He paid for his food and got up to leave. He had only just gotten to the door when he overheard a familiar disturbance.

Surely he was mistaken. But no, he turned around and like many of the other guests saw the man he was looking for arguing with his waiter. Just like he had been at the Northern Pioneer the other night. This time of course he wouldn't be interfering. He just stood back and saw how it played out.

The waiter wasn't taking it from the man and soon had a couple tough looking bouncers at his side. They took the man each by one arm and frog-walked him out of the club. There they dumped him unceremoniously on the curb. "This was your last warning." One of the bouncers informed him. "You are no longer welcome here." And with that they shut the door. Thatcher had exited as discreetly as he could. Now he stood in the shadows of the alley watching to see where his prey would go next.

The man rose to shaky feet and began a slow walk down the darkened street. He wasn't making too much progress so Stephen followed him with ease. After they had traveled a few blocks the man entered a run down apartment tenement. Probably where he lived. Most of the windows were darkened. But Stephen Thatcher saw one light up as he spied on the building. Sure enough in the window he could make out the man.

Now that he knew where the man lived he could come back better prepared. The Moon Man would soon be paying him a visit.

The next evening found the Moon Man standing atop the roof of the apartment building. Preparing to make his way in and with luck bring an end to this adventure. As silently as he could, he opened the door granting him access to the building and made his way down the hall and up a flight of stairs to the floor he was seeking. The hall he now walked down was conveniently darkened by the bulbs being burnt out. He had to watch his step as the floor was littered with all manner of refuse. He couldn't make out most of it and

"You are no longer welcome here."

he had the feeling that was probably for the best. He wasn't sure he wanted to know just what he was stepping around.

Finally he came to a door. The room number had long since fallen off. But that was okay as he knew from his surveillance the night before that this door corresponded with the rooms of the man he was looking for.

Moon Man quietly tried the knob. Not surprisingly he found it unlocked. The door opened with ease and he snuck into the room beyond. He closed the door behind him and moved swiftly through the shadows. No one was at home at the moment, just as he had hoped. He settled in to await the return of his prey.

It turned out that he didn't have too long to wait. Only moments later he heard the doorknob rattling. Moon Man drew himself up and prepared to strike when the time came. The man entering the apartment flipped on the lights as he came through the door. It was immediately that he saw he was not alone. The figure of the Moon Man loomed at him from across the room. A gun drawn and aimed straight at him. The man coming in had a bag of groceries that immediately dropped to the floor with a crash, milk and eggs spilling out at his feet.

They just stood there facing one another. The man could see his face reflected in the mirrored globe that was the Moon Man's head. He had no idea who was behind it or what they could want. But he was sure it was nothing good.

"You have been receiving documents that are not yours to receive."

"I don't know what you're talking about." He grew defiant, even in the face of the gun leveled at him. "I ain't received no documents from nobody."

"Dusk said otherwise. I've been tracking you down ever since."

"Don't know no 'Dusk'"

"Just the other evening you were dining at the Northern Pioneer when he and his men robbed the place." Moon Man drew closer. "But that was just a ruse. They were really there to hand off papers to you."

He realized there was no point in denying it anymore. Moon Man had him dead to rights. "What's it to you? From what I hear of you this ain't no business of yours."

"Just satisfying my curiosity."

"Not a good thing to be curious about. I have connections and this is well above you and your petty league. Best for you to just forget about me and my papers. You're liable to live a little longer and keep your little racket going."

While he'd been talking he had failed to notice how close Moon Man had been moving in. But now he realized it and tried to move back. He'd forgotten his spilled milk and slipped on it as he received a firm fist to the jaw. He tumbled to the floor and was out like a light.

When the man regained consciousness he was bound hand and foot to an old chair. The Moon Man loomed over him, his mirrored helmet gleaming in the dim light. "So tell me mister no name." Moon Man had as yet been unable to learn the man's identity. "Just what should I call you?"

"No Name." The man spat out. "You'll never learn anything."

"Fair enough No Name." Moon Man held up a series of photographs. "These men were heroes, yet you and your boss ruined them. Their reputations are destroyed. For one of them life itself has been destroyed."

"Yeah so? What's it to the likes of you?"

"I do what I must. My interest isn't what you should be concerned about. What I do to you is."

"Everybody in this town knows about you mister Moon Man. Just as you caught me, you'll get caught as well. One of these days."

"Perhaps." Moon Man shrugged. "But I doubt today is that day." He pulled up a chair and sat across from No Name. He wasn't sure just what he wanted to do next. Even through his helmet his indecision must have been perceivable. For No Name smirked.

Moon Man wiped the smirk off his face with another knock-out punch. Thinking it over he decided what he should do next. It wouldn't do for Moon Man to get the information out of him. But an anonymous tip leading to his arrest; that could work. The police questioning him would be far more effective. And No Name here could be brought to proper justice.

Stephen Thatcher stood in the hall waiting. He was somewhat anxious. Since they brought No Name in he had been waiting to hear from Detective Lt. Gil McEwen. He hoped that his partner had learned more than he had from the man. With luck they would be able to clear Dusk and Dawn and restore some of their tarnished reputation.

"Sergeant. Come quick sir." Patrolman Owens came running up to him. Looking quite upset and out of breath.

"What is it?"

"Down in lock-up. Dusk and Dawn, they've escaped." Thatcher's eyes widened. Not hesitating he followed the patrolman down to the lock-up. Sure enough he found the two cells where Dusk and Dawn were being held empty. Not a trace of them could be found. But how had they managed to pull it off? The cells remained locked and there seemed to be no evidence of any other escape route having been used. Yet, they were well and truly gone.

"How could they have gotten out?"

"The Moon Man?" Owens suggested. "They were working together at the airfield. Maybe they're in this together."

"Maybe. But I doubt it."

"Why not?" Owens narrowed his eyes as he watched the Sergeant.

"Moon Man has always operated alone. We've never had any evidence of him having accomplices before. Why start now?"

"I guess so."

Stephen Thatcher shook his head in wonder as he looked in the cell once more. He would need to tell Gil about this. And that was something he was not looking forward to. He made his way back up to McEwen's office head hung in disgust.

They discussed the situation. Since Dusk and Dawn escaped they had no grounds to hold No Name. He hadn't been forthcoming with any information as it was. And their only evidence against him was the word of two escaped convicts. McEwen had no choice but to let him go. Stephen Thatcher had to reluctantly agree, but he also knew that the Moon Man might want to follow up on this.

The next day found him meeting with his ally Angel once more. Though he needed to get back to his mission he also wanted to keep tabs on mister No Name. He should have thought about getting the man's name from Gil. But he'd been distracted by the escape of Dusk and Dawn and it never occurred to him. However, he now felt that they might decide to go after him as well. For his part in what had been done to them. Maybe he could kill two birds with one stone. If he could catch them together.

Of course No Name had packed up and left his old apartment. With luck Angel would be able to track down where he'd gone. As long as he had stayed in Great City that was. If he had skipped town there was nothing else they could do.

It took a couple of days but Angel was able to learn something. No Name was still in town, and he was up to something. He had been meeting with some mysterious men that no one knew anything about. That was something at least. And Angel had learned where they had been meeting. Moon Man decided that he would stake out the place and handle things as needed.

That night found him waiting outside what seemed to be an abandoned building. Windows had been boarded up and not a light shown. But the doors stood open and there was movement inside. Moon Man drew closer to investigate the best that he could. He could make out the shapes of several men moving around just inside. It was too dark to make them out clearly, but when one of them spoke he knew the voice immediately. It was No Name!

Good, he was right in choosing to be here tonight. He continued to observe them at a distance. But they went in where he could no longer see them. So he followed carefully. As he stood in the doorway he could tell they had moved upstairs.

Creeping through the gloom he made his way to the staircase. There was a dim light coming from the floor above. Moon Man crept up the stairs as quietly as he could. The faint creaks echoed loudly in his ears. Though he knew they weren't enough to be heard by the men above.

He arrived on the second floor and saw that they had moved on to a room at the far end of the hall. He had made it halfway there when there came a crash from the room. Hearing the gunshots that followed he broke into a run and burst through the door. Moon Man wasted no time going into action. No Name and his pals were fighting with Dusk and Dawn. Moon Man tackled the nearest of the men, knocking him into one of the others. This gave Dusk the opportunity to duck under the shot aimed at his head.

Dawn swept the legs from No Name and pounced on him. He began to pummel him about the face. Dusk grabbed one of the other men and threw him out the window. Moon Man could see they were out for blood. He slammed his foe against the wall and slugged him. The man slumped to the floor unconscious and Moon Man turned to face them.

The next one was cleverer and he held back as he pulled out a revolver and took aim. He had a clear shot, but he was too focused on Moon Man. Dusk clubbed him in the head with a pipe. He watched as the man's head caved in from the blow. This was not going how he had hoped. Dusk and Dawn were making things so much worse for themselves with each blow.

He moved to stop them, but Dusk gut punched him and he crumpled to the floor himself. "Sorry Moon Man, but you shouldn't have gotten involved in this."

A simple punch like that shouldn't have taken him out, but he felt himself blacking out. As the room grew blurry he could still make out some of what was being said. "...not sure why he's here but we'll leave him."

"Is that a good idea?"

"Maybe not. But I don't think we should kill him. Let's just deal with them."

There was more said but he didn't make any of it out. Moon Man was unconscious.

When he came to Moon Man found himself the only living person in the room. His helmet was still on and other than having been knocked out cold he was unharmed. No Name and his pals were all dead and there was no sign of Dusk and Dawn. They'd gotten their revenge and fled the scene.

"I guess I should report this and get Gil over here." On unsteady legs he made his way back out to his car and changed. Then he got to a nearby phone and called in to report that he had found the crime scene. Once he reported in he went back to keep an eye on things until Gil could arrive.

Gil stood behind his desk looking grim. Things had not turned out the way they had wanted. Not in the least.

No Name and his associates were all dead. Gil had discovered that the name he had gotten out of him had been false, so they still had no idea as of yet to who he had really been. Not only that, but Dusk and Dawn were still out there. If only they had cooperated with him. Then things might have gone better. But by busting out and then killing, no there would be no coming back from that.

"I don't get it." Gil fummed. "As if I didn't have enough to deal with in The Moon Man."

"They probably won't stick around Gil." Stephen told him. "They'll be someone else's problem."

"True." Gil agreed, "And we can focus back on that Moon Man."

"Number one priority." Stephen sighed inwardly. Things would be back to normal in Great City.

It was a long dark road that they drove on late into the night. With only the light of their headlamps breaking through the darkness. The two men had made it out of the city and were on their way, somewhere. Just away from Great City was the only thing for certain. Dusk shook his head as he peered through the darkness ahead of them. They could never go back there.

"Looks like we're fugitives now."

"I suppose so Sir. Maybe we shouldn't have busted out and did what we did."

"I have no regrets about how we handled things. We were out of luck already." He thought back to how it had all spiraled out of their control. Letting themselves get mixed up with those crooked agents. They probably weren't even government agents. Then they had that run-in with The Moon Man which had led up to their arrest. Moon Man may not have been working with the police, but he had still brought Dusk and his men to their attention. And it had cost one of them his life. And now the two of them, once war heroes were on the lam.

They focused on the road they were on. Dawn Larry was a good man and a loyal soldier. He would stick by his commander. And from now on they were on their own. Breaking out of jail and getting out of Great City hadn't been easy. Dusk had to use an old jail break trick he'd picked up during the war when they'd been held prisoner for a time. Then they had to avoid the law at every turn it seemed. But eventually they had managed to make it back to their airfield. Of course it wouldn't be theirs any more. Not staying for long they gathered up what they could and got in Dusk's car and set out on the road.

On through the night they drove, not once stopping. Just going on until day broke. Finally as the sun rose Dusk pulled off to the side of the road and waited. What was next for them he wondered as he tapped his fingers on the steering wheel. The two of them got out of the car, stretched their legs and walked around for a bit. It had been a long night and an even longer past few days. Things didn't look like they were going to get any easier.

After they were done they traded places and Dawn Larry took the wheel as they set out once more. He drove on until at last they reached a roadside diner. It wouldn't hurt to stop and get something to eat. They had changed out of their uniforms and were dressed a little more plainly. There was no need to draw any attention to themselves.

They went in and took a seat. A rather tired waitress came up and took their orders. They had enough money, they could afford a decent breakfast and they knew they needed it. They discussed their plans in hushed tones as they ate. They could hole up for a day or two maybe in the next town they reached. It was risky but they decided to take the chance. They should be able to trade in the car for something different. That would help to throw off any pursuit for a while at least. Then they could work on finding a way out of the country. Dusk still had contacts in Europe. If they could get back there they could get some help from them.

After they finished eating they returned to find several men in neat suits standing near their car. Government men from the look, they could tell. They were stern faced and appeared ready for a confrontation. One of them pushed back his coat to reveal his holster. He was clearly the man in charge here. Another shifted nervously behind him drawing his attention. A sideways glance from him and the man stiffened.

"Well, that's it then." Dusk knew there was no getting out of this. They were tired, unarmed and outnumbered. Another time they could have fought their way out of a situation like this. But not this time.

"If you gentlemen would please come with us."

Dusk and Dawn put up their hands. "Of course." The men came up with hand-cuffs and secured the two of them. They then led them towards a waiting car and shoved them in. One of the government men stayed behind and took their car and followed as they left.

"Well, you two have really been a headache for me." The man in charge informed them with a shake of his head. "But it was worth it in the end."

Dusk looked up puzzled. "What?"

"Thanks to your little exploits with that Moon Man fellah and the law a dangerous man has been brought down and his organization have been crippled." He explained, "I know you and your men were helpless patsies in the whole deal. You really believed you were working for us."

"So we weren't. So what?" Dusk wasn't sure just what was going on here. But he was getting frustrated by this man's attitude.

"So, there's a good chance I can change that." He motioned to one of his men who unlocked their hand-cuffs. "That is if you can be less of a headache."

Dusk shook his head. He'd been burned once by trusting and he wasn't sure he wanted to do it again. "No, sorry. Just lock us up."

Word got back to police headquarters about the recapture of Dusk and Dawn. Gil was pleased and Thatcher was relieved. They would have no more problems with those two it seemed.

"So, we got a tip." Gil informed Stephen. "Might be a good one. One that could lead us to Moon Man. We can get him once and for all."

"I'll get on it Gil." Stephen Thatcher assured him. Smiling inwardly, glad things were back to usual.

THE END

STORY INSPIRATION

*T*he idea for this story came about as I wondered what would happen when Moon Man encountered another pulp hero. Only this hero had gone down a bad path. No longer the good man he'd once been. I knew I didn't want to use an established character so I came up with Dusk and Dawn. They were based loosely on G-8 and his Battle Aces, favorites of mine.

To help me visualise what I was working with I drew up some sketches of them along with Moon Man himself. I kept the drawings handy while I wrote to help as I pictured the action in my head.

In the beginning I felt that they, Dusk and Dawn would be redeemed. But as the story progressed I could see that it wasn't to be. Dusk in particular had accepted the fact that they were crossing lines which they couldn't cross back. They'd gone too far and were going further. Even though they felt regret for their actions they knew there would be consequences. They made peace with that and when it became obvious that they couldn't escape those they accepted them.

A part of me was pulling for them as I wrote the story. I could see that it was as much about Dusk and Dawn as the Moon Man. But their story came to an end though Moon Man's will continue on.

J.L. LAMATUS is a writer, an artist and has worked as an assortment of jobs from retail to cook and janitor, not at the same time of course. His love of pulps began in high school when his neighbor loaned him Burroughs' Venus novels. Immediately hooked he has been reading and writing pulp stories ever since. J.L. can be quite nostalgic about things as can be seen on his blog at www.shadeofjeremy.com. He is also quite active on Twitter @shadeofjeremy and can be reached at sojdesigns@aol.com His author page at amazon.com/author/jllamastus has more info and other works.

LAWYERS FIRST
By Kevin Findley

Friday, Sep 7th, 1936

The four men in the warehouse gathered around a large crate. One watched the front entrance, while the others kept stealing a glance to the office on the opposite wall. Unlike many of the men standing around Great City, none of the clothes on these men were threadbare, and the few with patches were professionally done and barely noticeable.

"Hey, Donnie, how come the four of us are out here when the accountants got two of Lashky's best guns in there with them?" The one watching the door turned to answer the question.

"We're what the Army might call the first line of defense, Lenny. Course if you ask any drill sergeant, he'd tell you we're just the trip wire, so they have time to get the money out first."

"At least that spooky freak ain't here to wreck things." The blond man who spoke pulled out a deck of cards and looked around. Donnie shook his head, and he put them away.

"Naw, this guy ain't spooky, Bernie. He's one of those things out of that H.G. Wells book; an alien!"

"Oh come on, Lenny, you're digging stuff out of a forty-year-old book!"

"That's how the Brits covered up their invasion Donnie."

Everyone groaned at that. Lenny Dorsett had started seeing conspiracies everywhere since FDR took the country off the gold standard in '33. He thought the President's family was in league with greedy dentists to take everyone's gold and silver fillings, teeth, and bridges, replacing them with steel.

"So the Moon Man is an alien taking orders from King Edward?" Donnie Potts shook his head and grabbed Lenny by the shoulder. "You may be my cousin, but your pumpkin is lookin' more like a jack o' lantern."

"There ain't no need to talk like that Donnie. Of course, they're not working for him. The Limeys sent a few over here to work for Hoover so he can keep Roosevelt in check!"

Above them, the man preparing to leap down listened carefully. *They think I'm an alien? This ought to be interesting.*

After another minute of Lenny rambling on, Bernie Parks gave his own thoughts on Great City's resident bogeyman.

"He ain't no alien, even aliens bleed. This freak is a ghost!"

This is even better! Thought the man over their heads. He carefully checked his black cloak again to make certain it didn't catch on anything when he decided to leap down.

"Oh, come on, Bernie! How do you figure that?"

"There's a half-dozen guys that said they shot him point-blank and no blood, not a drop. How do you explain that?"

The cloak makes them miss, and no one's ever gotten closer than eight or ten feet for a shot. I've got a couple of them that look like a slice of Swiss cheese though. The helmeted figure grimaced and rubbed his shoulder. *The only guy who ever shot at me and hit was Gil.*

"Those guys are making it up. They just don't want to admit they can't shoot straight."

"Then how does he get out of every jam he's ever walked into?"

"I don't know, but a ghost passes through everything. Jimmy from over on 49th got hit so hard; he lost two teeth. No ghost can throw a punch like that."

"Of course a ghost can throw a punch, it's just a matter of controlling his, whatchacallit, ectoplasm!"

"Now you're starting to sound like one of those weird tales from the radio!"

The fourth man around the crate, Frankie Geitzler, began to speak.

"You're both nuts. He's not a ghost or an alien; he's a whole gang of guys."

"How do you figure that?"

"We've never seen him right? That helmet on his head twists his voice up, right? I've talked to enough guys that got a hand on him to know he's got two arms and two legs."

"What about blood?"

"A couple of guys from the Purple Gang swear he bleeds, one of 'em stuck the knife in himself."

OK, that did happen. The hood barely got his blade in between a couple of ribs, but there was blood on the knife when he pulled it back.

"So what was under the cloak?"

"He didn't see any skin, said the guy's got a full suit on under there. One of 'em could even be a colored guy, and we'd never know it."

That might be useful. The Lunar Avenger glanced toward the front of the warehouse. *It's about time for Angel to make a distraction.*

Moments later, a loud thwacking sound drew everyone's attention, and then the lights went out in the warehouse. As the group of thugs turned toward the sound, the Moon Man quietly stepped off the beam and jumped onto the crate he and Angel had moved into place earlier that day.

Bernie looked back as the Lunar Avenger landed on the crate. With the lights out, the only illumination was the moonlight reflected on the helmet of Great City's Robin Hood. He never saw the foot that kicked out and caught him under the chin.

Frankie jumped out of the way and tried to pull a short-barrel .38 out of his coat pocket. He almost had a shot lined up when a sharp slap on the back of his hand made him drop the gun. As he glanced down for his fallen weapon, a blow to his temple dropped him to the ground.

Lenny and Donnie turned into each other and smacked foreheads hard enough to stun them both. The two cousins looked at the spectral sight before them and ran for the exit.

With the other guards down and out of the way, the Moon Man moved toward the small, walled-in office area. As he approached, he heard the distinctive sound of a bolt being pulled back and barely ducked down and to the left before a stream of .45 slugs tore past and into the post in front of him.

When the shooting stopped, he moved silently around the wood support beam and fired three quick shots into the middle of the hole pattern now stitched through the plywood door. Dropping quickly back behind the post again, it took only a moment to hear a cry of pain and then the sound of a body falling to the floor.

One down, one to go!

He waited a few seconds and then moved toward the door again. The Moon Man could hear air moving through the holes in it. Confused at first, he then realized that the back of the office was also the back of the warehouse. In frustration, he kicked open the door to find the body of the gunman he killed on the ground, and a bolt hole cut through the wall. Light from the street lamp shined inside.

The Moon Man quickly ducked and dove through the hole into the alley behind the warehouse. He rose to see a sedan at the end of the alley turn sharp left, lifting it almost onto two wheels. Returning to the office, he removed a flashlight from a clip on his belt, switched it on, and looked around the abandoned office where he found a large bag a few feet from the gunman and his fallen Thompson.

"Well, at least it wasn't a total loss for Great City charities tonight." The canvas bag, like one used by any one of the hundreds of men down on their luck, held a large amount of cash. A quick look revealed that it was mostly ones and twos, but the Moon Man could also see a few fivers and even a ten spot mixed in.

"I guess they already counted the big bills and took them when they bolted." He muttered.

Hearing footsteps, he looked up and shined his flashlight to see Ned "Angel" Dargan walk into the office. The former boxer pulled down the balaclava mask covering the lower half of his face, revealing a nose repeatedly broken in the ring and looked down at the money bag. Angel unconsciously rubbed his knuckles as he spoke.

"The ones that ran didn't get far, Boss."

"Did you cut the phone lines too, Angel?" Shortly after Stephen revealed his real name to Angel, both men agreed not to use them when "on-the-job".

"No, only the power."

"Good, I have to call Gil and let him know to send out the meat wagon."

"Paddy wagon too. I remembered to tie them up this time."

The Moon Man laughed as he dialed Gil's office. The police lieutenant picked up before the first ring finished.

"McEwen here."

Roughing up his voice a little more, the man beneath the Argus globe spoke. "Good evening, Lieutenant. I have a few rivals for you to pick up. Don't worry; most of them are still alive this time."

"I'm not your errand boy, you loony crook! If you're so worried about the competition, drop them off yourself. I'll have plenty of handcuffs to go around."

"Not a chance Lieutenant, I believe every story I've ever heard about how tough you are. That's why I'm making sure you don't have enough time to catch me." He let McEwen curse him for a few moments, then spoke again.

"Everyone is ready for collection at a warehouse near Douglas and Adams. You know the one, it belongs to Lashky." McEwen let go with one more curse and then slammed down the phone.

"Let's go, Angel. If Gil isn't here in five minutes, I'll grill and eat this cloak like a porterhouse."

As Angel drove down the darkened avenues, the Lunar Avenger quickly removed his helmet and cloak, revealing the handsome face of Great City Police Sergeant Stephen Thatcher. With a sharp turn of his hands, he separated the two halves of the globe, wrapped them in the cloak, placed them inside an ordinary, athletic bag, and threw the gloves from his disguise on top.

Stephen looked over the money in the canvas bag and set it aside. After he almost passed on several bills with blood on them a few weeks ago, both men agreed to have Angel inspect everything before giving it to a local charity or mailing it anonymously back to the rightful owner.

"How's it going back there, Stephen?"

"I'm good, Ned." The plainclothes sergeant told his partner about the conversation before the lights went out as he removed his badge, service revolver, wallet, and keys from the pocket on the back of the driver's seat, and placed them in his jacket pockets. Then he dropped the canvas money bag onto the front seat with Angel.

"Sounds like everyone has their own idea about the Moon Man."

"That's good. It keeps them from working together." Angel nodded in agreement.

"Okay then, we already talked about the orphanage partner, so where else am I visiting this weekend?"

"The First Baptist Church soup kitchen could use a hand."

Angel nodded. "There's also that family shelter over on Singer Street. Julie told me the City Council wants to start pulling back money since they think the economy is going great now." Julie Pascal worked for Great City Family Services. After a month of looking askew at Ned Dargan's scarred face, she finally saw the heart underneath, and the two began dating in August.

"Right." Stephen grimaced. "That's got to be Deputy Mayor Evans behind that. His family has a finger in every dirty pie in the city."

Theodore Evans II was the third generation of an already spoiled, useless family of the Great City hoi polloi who specialized in shoving everyone else away from the trough of city contracts and other public money. Remembering a family rivalry reported on the high society page, Stephen leaned over the seat.

"Who runs that family shelter?"

"The Vandergilt family; they also handle a lot of the …" Angel suddenly stopped, looked in the rearview mirror, and started laughing.

"I got it now. If we hand the money over to the Vandergilt operations, the family can spread their money around more. Then it won't matter if the Council pulls their money and whatever Evans' family wants with those properties ain't going to happen."

"That's the idea, Ned."

"I know the night manager at the shelter and a couple of people at Vandergilt's food bank. That ought to get me in to see the right people to hand out a few donations."

After the Crash, Preston Aloysius Vandergilt did everything possible to keep his businesses open and his people employed. Rumor had it that he used up more than half of the family fortune before the economy started to turn around.

When the old man died in '35, it was the largest funeral turnout since the Lincoln Train stopped in Great City. Preston's daughter, Irene, was keeping up her Father's legacy. When the Moon Man decided it was time to "rob the rich and give to the poor", he felt the Vandergilts were already paid up in his ledger.

The Evans family, on the other hand, fired everyone they could after the Crash, and cut pay to near starvation wages for the employees they kept, nearly all of whom fled at the first, better opportunity. The family never fully recovered its former financial and social glory, which rankled Deputy Mayor Evans to no end.

"We're almost there." Angel soon turned the car onto the street on the west side of the gymnasium that many of the cops in Great City used in the fight against too many doughnuts during the day and too much beer after the end of their shift at night.

"Take care, partner." Stephen grabbed the handle and started to exit the sedan.

"You want the total count before I start shifting around the take?"

Stephen winced. "I wish you wouldn't call it that."

Dargan grinned back at him from the driver's seat.

"Okay partner, I'll phone you tomorrow."

"Just let me know whenever you can."

After checking that no one else was in the parking lot, Stephen jumped out and walked quickly to his car. Anyone looking out of the gym windows or pulling into the parking lot now would only see someone heading to their car after a workout. As Stephen got into his auto, Angel pulled out of the alley and headed for his walk-up apartment.

Sue McEwen was waiting for Stephen when he walked through his front door. She moved quickly to embrace her fiancé as he dropped the athletic bag and closed the door behind them.

"How did it go tonight, darling?"

"Smoothly for once, Sue. We certainly hurt Lashky; maybe not so much with the money we took from his bookkeepers, but one of his button men went down, and a whole nest of thugs are wearing cuffs right now."

Sue moved to the sofa, slipped off her Mary Janes and tucked her feet underneath as she sat down. Stephen emptied his pockets on the hall table then joined her.

"Angel went home to check the money, and he'll start distributing it to the Great City Orphanage and a few other charities around town." Stephen left out how close the Tommy gun came, but told his fiancée everything else. Sue knew better, however.

"Right, everything went just your way, and all the bad guys did was shoot rubber bands at you."

Stephen felt his face burn like a schoolboy, but, blue eyes flashing, refused to back down. He launched into the same speech he gave whenever Sue wanted him to put aside the globe of his lunar alter-ego. She listened for about a minute and then got up to switch on the radio. Hoagie Carmichael's *One Morning in May* quickly filled the apartment.

"I didn't mean to get you angry, Stephen, and you know I'll support you however long you decide to wear that helmet. You must realize, though, that you are going to have to stop this. Dad is going to figure you out, and the only way he won't arrest you is if you quit first and then tell him everything before he puts two and two together." As she spoke, Sue carefully ran her fingers over Stephen's short brown hair, only a few shades darker than her own.

Her father, the same Lieutenant Gil McEwen the Moon Man called earlier, had been Stephen's training officer when he was a rookie, and happily took the young man on again as part of his Plainclothes Unit once he made sergeant.

Gil never cut him slack, despite Stephen's father being the Deputy Chief of Police back then. His philosophy, as Gil explained it once, and only once, was simple.

"Everyone is going to think you got here because of your old man. If you want to prove everybody wrong, including yourself, that means you have to outshoot, outfight, and outsmart everyone else in Great City. Fortunately, I'm the one man who can help you do that."

Gil certainly lived up to his word. Stephen thought with a grin.

Feeling she had made her point, Sue changed the subject as she sat down again.

"Is Ned going by the orphanage with his charity's donation in the morning or wait to have lunch with the kids?"

"If there is a chance Julie Pascal is there in the morning on business, you couldn't keep him away with a Studebaker."

"What if I was there, Steve?" She asked with a questioning look in her brown eyes.

"You couldn't pull me away with one of those new auto gyros."

"Good answer!" Sue slid across the middle cushion of the sofa, leaned in close, and kissed him good and long.

Ringgggggg! Steve slowly pulled away from Sue and reached for the phone on the end table.

"Hello?"

"It's Gil, Steve."

"Aw come on, Gil! It's still my day off."

"My watch says it's 12:01 am on a Saturday. Now turn off Carmichael, turn loose of my daughter, and pay attention."

Without realizing it, Stephen quickly removed his other arm and nearly sat up at attention. Sue smothered her laughter with both hands and moved across her fiancé's small living room to turn off the radio.

Saturday, Sep 8th

Angel looked up at Great City Orphanage with a wry grin on his pug face as he climbed the steps to the entrance. He had a few good memories from the short time he spent here after his parents died, but only a few. Fortunately, his first trainer saw him in a scrap in the playground behind the building, took him in, and introduced him to the ring that made up the center of his life before his arm injury two years ago.

After a few more seconds on Memory Lane, Angel walked in and quickly knocked on Althea Dalton's office door.

"Come in!"

"Hi, Mrs. Dalton. How are the kids today? Is …" The question about Julie died on his lips as Angel laid eyes on the most beautiful woman he ever saw sitting across from the orphanage director.

"Hello, Ned!" Dalton stood up and came around her desk to embrace the former boxer. Althea looked about twenty years younger than her actual age of sixty, and still had the energy needed to corral fifty-two children from the ages of five to seventeen.

"How are you, young man?"

"I'm doin' just fine."

"Well of course you are." She turned toward the woman seated near them.

"I'd like to introduce you to Miss Irene Vandergilt."

"I'll leave now Althea." She got up quickly. "You obviously have a delivery to accept."

"Mr. Dargan is the former boxer and regular donor we were just speaking about Irene."

Angel broke free of the hug and dropped an envelope on her desk.

"Here's a little something from the Retired Boxer's Association, Mrs. Dalton."

Irene shook her head and closed her eyes for a moment.

"I apologize Mr. Dargan. That was presumptuous of me."

Angel just smiled at her. "That's okay Miss Vandergilt. You obviously have more important mugs than me to meet today; maybe even an actual deliveryman or two."

To his surprise, the 'high-society dame' actually laughed at the jab and stuck her hand out.

"Fair enough Mr. Dargan. Perhaps we'll meet at the next fundraiser."

Angel took the proffered hand in his own and was surprised at the firm grip.

Next time I leave money at her Singer Street shelter, I'm giving it to her personally!

"I'll have to buy a monkey-suit, but I'll be there."

Irene laughed again, released his hand, and went toward the office door with a wave to Mrs. Dalton.

"Henry should be outside with the car, so I'll say good-bye now Althea. I look forward to next week."

Once the door closed, Althea put her hands on her hips and looked at Angel.

"You simply can't talk to a member of one of Great City's first families like that Ned. She is used to a much more refined type of conversation."

"Is that so Mrs. Dalton? I get the feeling she can give as good as she gets. Probably trades punches pretty well too." Althea merely tapped her foot in irritation for a moment before changing the subject.

"You really should register your organization with the city. Then you could go public with all of your good works."

"I'm fine without all the fuss, Mrs. Dalton." Angel also didn't want to have to reveal that less than half of the dollars he gave her came from other boxers. No matter how he got it, Althea would not take what she thought was money rooted in the sins that eventually sent so many children to her doors. Before she could push the point, Angel asked about the real reason he came to the orphanage so early.

"Is Julie around this morning?"

"I'm sorry no; she's working out of her office today. Would you like to visit the children?"

Angel waved her off. "No thanks, I remember what it's like lining up for some visitor when your stomach is grabbing you by the ribs, reminding you that you ain't had any breakfast yet."

The former light-weight excused himself and walked outside just in time to see Vandergilt's driver punch a man in the jaw as another one came up behind him and a third tried to open the passenger door. Irene sat in the back, looking worried for her driver, but not at all scared.

As the driver went down from a blow to the neck, Angel leaped off the stairs and walked to the big sedan, slapping his feet on the sidewalk to get their attention. The one who sucker-punched the driver sneered at the shorter man.

"Buzz off shrimp. This ain't your business."

Angel closed the gap with the red-haired thug and with two steps left, moved in so quickly, the goon missed it as he blinked. Then the former contender's hard, right hand buried itself in Red's gut, and bent him double instantly.

The thug trying to open the door barely got his mitt off the handle before Angel buried a left in his right side and then followed up with a right jab to the chin that snapped his head back and sent him stumbling until he tripped off the curb and fell.

Angel was already turning back to Red as the man tried to get up. He grimaced as he kicked the man in the ribs, putting him back on the ground. Kicking a man went against Angel's training, but working with the Moon Man the last two years had taught him the value of making sure a mook didn't get up when there was more than one of them to knock down.

He spun around, grabbed the man getting off the street by the tie, and wrapped it around his neck. Angel then pulled the now choking thug over to the still running auto blocking Vandergilt's car, and slammed his head into the right, rear door.

"Grab him!" The thug by Vandergilt's car looked up to see Angel pointing at the one still out cold from the driver's blow. "Pull him into this heap and get out." He looked back to see Red's eyes start to clear.

Angel grabbed him by the ear, bounced him off the rear bumper, and threw him into the backseat beside the unconscious thug and slammed the door closed the same moment as the third thug got behind the wheel. Once the car pulled away, Angel turned to help Vandergilt's driver to his feet.

"You okay pal?"

The driver looked back at his boss, who nodded her head up and down. He turned back to Angel. "I'm good, thanks for jumping in there." He stuck out his hand which Angel quickly took.

"That was a swell punch, guy never woke up."

"Thanks, I ..." He stopped as Vandergilt interrupted them.

"Mister Dargan, may I speak with you?" Angel nodded at the driver and walked to the window as Irene finished rolling it down.

"Thank you for assisting Henry. I don't know what those men wanted, but I'm certain it wasn't an invitation to brunch."

"You're welcome Miss Vandergilt." Angel looked back at the retreating automobile. "Maybe I should have held onto one of them."

"No, if you had done that, Mrs. Dalton would have insisted on calling the Police. That might have brought unwelcome attention to the orphanage." Henry climbed in and sat behind the wheel as she spoke.

"Yeah, I guess you're right about that." For Dargan, the orphanage was the closest thing he had to family before joining forces with Stephen Thatcher and

...a right jab to the chin that snapped his head back...

his globed alter-ego. He'd do anything to protect it and the children living there.

"May I extend my own invitation to you to Sunday brunch tomorrow Mr. Dargan? I would make it today of course, but I'm already engaged through the afternoon."

"That ain't necessary Miss Vandergilt. I'm always happy to slap around a few guys that don't know how to treat a lady like yourself."

"Please Mr. Dargan, I insist. Besides, I have an ulterior motive."

"Well that's fine Miss Vandergilt," Angel responded with a straight face, "but you're going to have to tell me what an ulterior is first."

As the driver nearly choked trying not to laugh, Irene gave Angel the fisheye and handed him a card. "Show that to the gate guard at 10:30 tomorrow morning and he will tell you where to park. The address is on the back." She tapped her hand on the front seat. "Let's go home Henry."

"Yes ma'am!" He gave Angel a half salute. "See you tomorrow Pal!"

Angel looked at the car as it pulled away and then down at the card in his hand.

"Why do I get the feeling I was better off with the thugs?" Angel muttered to himself.

Pocketing the card, he went to his own sedan and tried to guess if Julie might want to go to lunch. There were no clients wanting boxing lessons until next Wednesday, so the $2 bill in his wallet had to last another four days. He figured the café near Julie's office would be OK.

After all, a guy's gotta eat!

As Stephen walked up the precinct house steps, he couldn't shake Sue's words from last night. He knew Gil, and his Father, wanted the Moon Man off the streets of Great City and would be disappointed in him, no matter what argument he gave them. They might regret having to arrest him, but they would still handcuff him as fast as any other crook.

Not telling Gil was almost as hard as keeping the truth from his father. Both men had seen Great City nearly tear itself apart in the worst days of the Depression, and viewed the still growing division between the poor and the rich as one of the reasons Great City and much of the country was not recovering as quickly as it should.

Even Sweden came out of its worst days in '34. Stephen thought.

It was why he decided to adopt the identity of the Moon Man. The same reason, though, often gave him pause to reconsider why he put on the globe since he found himself also dealing out a more personal form of justice than he was allowed to under the law.

The poor will always be with you. A reminder so important, it was in three of the Four Gospels. Stephen knew that meant there would always be a reason to keep wearing the helmet; it was up to him to put it down.

Perhaps it's getting close to that time. Gil's hatred for the Moon Man as a criminal was growing and starting to border on obsession. At first, it was fun to tweak McEwen's nose since it was a rare criminal in Great City that the tough lieutenant couldn't catch.

Sue is right. I'll have to retire the Moon Man completely before I could ever tell Dad or Gil about why I did this.

As he walked in the door, Stephen shook off his musings and headed straight for the office of the Plainclothes Unit. As usual, Gil was already there with a lit cigar clamped between his teeth. McEwen looked every one of his fifty-plus years. Unlike most men his age, those years didn't seem to age him, but rather tempered him like good steel.

"Bout time you showed Steve. You're only twenty minutes early."

"Some of us need more than three hours of sleep each night, Gil."

"A strong cup of coffee and a good cigar takes care of that."

"I'll believe that the day you start smoking good cigars."

Gil grinned at the jab, blew a huge cloud of smoke at Stephen, and tossed a copy of Judge Harold's order to him. The younger man sat down to read the order. He quickly finished and looked up incredulously.

"I didn't want to believe you last night, but here it is." Stephen tossed the copy back on Gil's desk.

"There's no reason for Judge Harold to sign-off on this."

Gil nodded in agreement.

"I never thought he was in anyone's pocket, but I'm about to change my mind. I was there when that junior shyster Everett was making his case."

"Hammond's favorite errand boy is the one slumming just to ask a few phony questions?" Stephen was immediately suspicious.

"Yep, he showed up just before you got here. The Assistant DA is watching him like a hawk."

Gil stabbed toward Stephen with the cigar.

"He didn't even claim he was looking for new information, just that there were discrepancies in the testimony. Harold didn't even wait to hear what lie Everett had prepared, he just ordered the D.A. to bring in Toller this morning."

Vincent Toller was a bookkeeper for Meyer Lashky. The crime boss was nicknamed 'Mercy' for the quality he never showed to anyone unless he decided to put a guy he was torturing out of his misery with a bullet in the temple. Toller mistakenly witnessed one of those rare moments two months ago and ran to the D.A. as fast as his bowlegs could carry him.

Lashky's lawyer, Mitchell Davis Hammond, had thrown up every roadblock to Toller's testimony and to suppress the ledgers he brought with him, but the trial was finally going in front of a jury in two weeks. Vincent had been in protective custody for the last month after his car mysteriously caught fire while under his carport.

"How did you know to be at the Judge's office?"

"For once, the DA asked us to be there. If I had to guess, I'd say it had more to do with irritating Duncan Everett and his boss than actually wanting our help."

Twenty minutes later, the interview was over, and Everett came out looking smug.

"Have a nice day, boys!" He shouted to everyone as he left the precinct.

McEwen looked at the Desk Sergeant, who immediately picked up the phone.

"What is he doing Gil?"

"Murphy there is dialing up the desk sergeant over at the 14th."

Getting no answer, Steve pushed ahead. "Why?"

Gil sighed. "The junior shyster lives just a few blocks from the precinct building. Next time he comes out of his house, he'll see an officer giving him a ticket for two broken taillights."

"Some people would call that petty Gil."

"Someone else might call it criminal abuse of power."

Stephen and Gil both spun around on their heels to face the only man who could put the fear of God into both of them, Peter Thatcher; Chief of the Great City Police Department and Stephen's Father.

"Make certain Hanlon at the 14th uses one of those street urchins he keeps collecting." The elder Thatcher stepped closer to Gil and pushed a finger hard into his chest. "Then, be sure I never hear about something like that again." Peter's blue eyes flashed sparks for a moment, and then he turned to his son.

"What about you, Stephen? You going to let this go without reporting it?"

"There's nothing to report Chief. You already know all about it and are choosing to ignore it."

Gil looked like he'd just swallowed one of his cigars as the Chief looked at his son with a sad face.

"Supporting your partner is a good thing, Son. However, you don't have to sound like a politician when you do it." He started to turn away and then changed his mind. "Make certain to show up for Sunday dinner. Bring your fiancée and her old man along. For now, go help the DA's watchdogs get Toller ready to travel back to his hotel." Thatcher left them still at attention and whistled his way back to his office.

A few minutes later, Stephen watched as Toller departed with his escort. The Assistant D.A. responsible for Toller's cooperation walked with him upstairs to the Plainclothes Unit.

"So tell me how it went Stan." Gil offered one of his cigars to Stanley Knox. He declined but lit up one of his own cigarettes.

"Easy, Lt. McEwen. So easy, it makes me wonder why Everett was really there."

"You think he was passing along a threat?" Stephen asked.

"I'd bet on it, but everything he asked or commented on was directly related to our case."

"You're certain about that?"

"Absolutely. I was keeping a close eye on them both. Nothing Lashky's attorney said got a reaction out of Vincent."

Gil leaned back in his chair, slowly drawing in smoke and blowing it toward the ceiling.

"It could be that Hammond is just trying to rattle Toller before going to court next week. I've seen him do it before."

"If that was it Gil, it failed. Vincent was rock solid."

The three men compared notes for a few more minutes, caught up on several old cases, and then Knox left for his office.

Sunday, Sep 9th

"Good Morning! How are things?" Angel handed Vandergilt's card to the gate guard who looked at him like he had a third eye growing out of his forehead, and certainly didn't belong this close to the Vandergilt mansion.

"I'm Mr. Dargan; here to meet Miss Vandergilt."

The guard pointed inside with his chin.

"Go around the right side there and park in the covered area next to the garage."

"You got it!" *Nothing like a guy who rides his rich boss' coattails.*

Angel quickly pulled around as directed and parked. As he got out of the sedan, he heard a familiar voice call, "Welcome to brunch, Pal!"

Angel turned to see Henry walking toward him.

"Good to see you." Angel grinned at him. "How's the neck?"

"I'm fine, if that thug had hit me a little higher, I could have shrugged it off and knocked him down too."

"Ha! That was my best feature in the ring. I once won a fight because the other guy broke a hand on my forehead."

Henry nodded toward the mansion. "Miss Vandergilt is waiting, let's talk on the way in."

As they headed toward the house, Angel asked, "How is she?"

"Solid as a rock. I've been here since she was twelve, and Miss Vandergilt has always had the same nerves." The driver spoke with more than a little pride in his boss.

"I don't think she'd get rattled if you pointed a gun at her."

"What does she want with me?"

"I'm not sure." Henry scratched his right ear. "She plays her cards close to the vest until she's ready to lay out the whole plan. Her father was the same way."

"So what am I supposed to do then?"

"That's easy, enjoy some of the best grub you'll ever eat in your life and listen to what she has to say." Henry stopped walking and looked at Angel.

"You know how to eat like a swell don't you?"

"Sure thing, the orphanage drilled that into us. The director back when I was a kid, Agatha Harker, wanted to make sure we didn't look like a bunch of hooligans in front of potential parents or embarrass her in front of a rich donor."

Henry started walking again.

"You'll be fine then, just don't drink those Mimosas faster than Miss Vandergilt."

"Why, is she going to try and keep up?"

"No." Henry laughed. "You'll slide off your chair trying to keep up with her!"

This brunch just got a lot more interesting.

"That was probably the best breakfast, excuse me, brunch, I've had since the last time I won a fight and could break training. Not to mention drinking in the morning." Angel reached into his coat pocket for the envelope of cash he had earmarked for the shelter and food bank. As he did, he saw the waiter start to move toward him, but Irene waved him off.

"If I had known you would be at Althea's office yesterday, I'd have given this to you then." He slid the envelope over to Irene who moved it to the edge of the table. The waiter looked more horrified than before, and quickly removed the offending item from the dining table.

"I didn't mean to give Jeeves there a heart attack, that's for your family's shelter."

"Thank you Mr. Dargan. Now, if you don't mind, I'll move on to my ulterior motive."

"Go ahead Miss Vandergilt."

"Now that the country is slowly doing better, there are other problems we're going to face."

"Like what? More jobs and better pay?"

"Those jobs and pay can bring our people back, but they also bring in folks from other cities and states still struggling." She raised one manicured hand and began counting off her points.

"First, more unaccompanied men and fewer in number but still more families. That means housing is going to be at a premium and rents are going to rise faster than many people can afford them."

"Second, with the improved economy, factories and other businesses can afford to hire adults and will start firing the children they've been working like adults. A few have already started, and that can leave some families without an income again."

"Third, there are ..." Vandergilt said before Angel cut her off.

"I get it Miss Vandergilt; the old problems may get solved, but we've got a carload of new problems about to run us over."

The heiress smiled at Angel's turn of phrase.

"That's it in a nutshell Mr. Dargan. The city council doesn't see it that way, however. They are ready to end all of the welfare programs so they can start lining their pockets at pre-Depression levels again."

"I'll bet they're looking at buildings they couldn't give away last year very differently now too."

Vandergilt blinked in surprise at the insightful response.

He's already been thinking on these lines. I need to stop underestimating Mr. Dargan!

"Exactly, we've got shelters and soup kitchens about to close unless someone pays up on options to buy the properties outright."

Angel leaned forward, putting both elbows on the table.

"How much to keep everything open?"

"Cheap, especially compared to prices prior to September of 1929. That's more than I can manage by myself; but I already have donors and partners in place for the properties. That's not why I asked you here, however."

"Then what's the $64 question?"

"While buying up these buildings is important; I also realize that we need a different type of orphanage to deal with these children."

I don't think I like where this is going. Angel thought to himself.

"You see, Mrs. Dalton has spoken of you several times. She agrees that I need someone who understands what it is to find themselves on the streets, with no family to support them. If they were the income source as I mentioned, then we'll see more families broken up. They'll be harder in spirit and more difficult to pull away from the lure of so-called 'easy money'."

She leaned forward, looking Angel directly in the eyes.

"I want you to run the orphanage."

Angel put down his Mimosa and looked at his host.

"I'm no administrator Miss Vandergilt. You need to have Althea make a recommendation."

"She already did; she just didn't realize it at the time."

"Even so, I can't ..."

"Please understand Mr. Dargan, I want to hire you because you know what these kids have gone through. Even more important, is the fact that you can show them that there is life after being in such an institution. Success, even."

"I can do that by coming by every week to give a pep talk."

"Come now Mr. Dargan. You know that only reaches the kids who haven't already given up and now only want to be like the thug down the street with a flashy suit and a few extra dollars in his pocket for their future." She gave him the same fisheye as yesterday.

"You can imagine what girls trapped in this situation think of the future."

"I get all that, but I never finished school. I can barely tell a ledger from a ledge or a ..."

"I wouldn't expect you to; in fact, I already have your assistant director already picked out."

"Yeah? Who would that be?"

Irene grinned like a cat with a couple of canary feathers still caught in its teeth.

"Julie Pascal."

Geez! I'd swear this girl just rang my bell like Eddie McNulty did back in '32!

"You got my attention Miss Vandergilt. Tell me what you have in mind for these kids."

Sunday Evening Sep 9th

"Is it too late to call Anita now?" Toller walked out of the bedroom where he had been reading.

Paretti looked up from his newspaper. The police officer glanced at the clock on the mantle and nodded. The last 24 hours went smoothly for Toller and his detail. Once Frank Paretti and Charles Klaffke got Vincent back in his hotel, the bookkeeper calmed down considerably.

"Go ahead, Vincent. You'll have to get used to checking in if you're going to marry that girl."

The bookkeeper just grinned, sat down on the sofa, and started dialing.

"It's worth it, Frank."

Paretti laughed and shook his head.

"Hello?" Asked a contralto voice.

"Hi, Anita."

"Vincent? Is everything OK?"

"Absolutely, darling. One little hiccup yesterday, but it's over with, and everyone here has been swell."

"I'm glad, dear. Oh, mother called again. She wants to come to visit us before the wedding."

"Never thought I could find a reason to be happy for this trial until now."

"Vincent! Now you know my mother loves you."

"Oh sure, that's why she invites one of your old boyfriends to the house whenever we visit her."

"Pish, Posh!"

"Language, Anita! Mother Newman might have your roommate listening at the door!"

"Very funny Vincent. Now if you're going to be this way, you might as well say 'Good Night.'"

"All right dear. There's nothing else to say anyway. I just wanted to hear your voice. Good night."

"Good night, darling."

As Toller put down the receiver, Charles spoke up from his chair by the radio, weapon out and on the table between him and the front door. He and Frank had worked with the D.A. for almost a year, and never had a problem with a witness, but neither officer wanted to be the first ones either.

"You look a little shook, Vincent. How long do you think you'll be on the outs?"

Toller got up from the sofa and stretched. "I just implied that her mother isn't one of the Blessed Saints. I figure it's going to be chilly from now until Halloween; maybe even Thanksgiving."

"Thank you for having us over Chief."

"For goodness sake, Sue! You'll be my daughter-in-law soon, so start calling me Peter or Pops, or something else, please!"

"All right then Pops." Sue glided over and hugged her future father-in-law quickly. As she did, the elder Thatcher looked over at Gil.

"It's still Chief to you."

McEwen held up his hands in surrender.

"I wouldn't have it any other way Boss!" He handed a bottle of wine to Stephen and hung his hat on the hall coat-rack.

"Thanks for picking out the wine Sue."

"How do you know I didn't pick it out?" Gil asked.

"Because it's older than last month."

"Ha!" The elder Thatcher laughed as Sue rolled her eyes.

"I'm going into the kitchen to make certain you haven't switched any major ingredients Pops. Since you three always talk business, get it out of your system now. Once I put food on the table, any mention of police business by one of you gets all three a lap full of gravy."

With that, Sue went into the kitchen. She knew Steve would tell her everything, and after Chief Thatcher once changed out peaches with bell peppers in a cobbler, she made certain that his meals were edible before they hit the table.

At least he likes to cook. I wouldn't trust Stephen not to burn down the kitchen.

"So tell me the rest of the story on Toller."

Peter rarely smoked at the dinner table, but made an exception this time. As he filled his pipe, Stephen laid out everything that happened with Gil stepping in occasionally to expand on a point or two.

"I wish we had something more to add, but that's it, Dad."

"Okay then." The elder Thatcher turned to Gil.

"Give me your first gut response."

"This is Hammond's play, whatever is going on. Lashky would rather put himself in front of a precinct of cops as witnesses to kill Toller rather than let a lawyer play footsie for him."

"So there's no chance Lashky is just using Hammond's law firm as a beater to drive him into the open?" Peter asked.

Gil shook his head no as Sue started bringing in the meal.

"Lashky's got a twisted sense of responsibility. He protects his organization like it was family since his mother died five years ago. Mercy will use that shyster in the courtroom, but he won't bother with Hammond outside of it."

As he started to continue, Sue quickly moved to her father's side, tipping the gravy boat so Gil could see it was full and still bubbling.

"Dad, you're first." She warned.

"Yes dear." Gil had the grace, not to mention sense, to look embarrassed.

With the threat of a burned lap in retreat, Stephen changed the subject to baseball, which quickly set McEwen and the elder Thatcher at each other over the merits of the Tigers versus the Nationals.

That'll keep 'em so busy, I'll have seconds before they can finish cutting up their pork chops. After all, a guy's gotta eat!

Monday, September 10th

Ringggg!!! Ringggg!!!

Stanley Knox nearly leaped to the ceiling and ran to the phone on his kitchen wall.

I have to stop falling asleep in that chair.

After fumbling the receiver, Knox finally got it to his ear and yawned until his jaw popped. Before he could say hello, the caller jumped in.

"It's Paretti. Toller just skipped out on us … wait for a second, I hear …" The officer's next words were lost to Knox with a crashing sound, shouting, and then the exchange of gunfire.

"Paretti! Paretti!" Knox waited five seconds, then ended the call and dialed for McEwen's office. The extension was picked up by the precinct switchboard operator who sent him to the front desk.

"This is Knox from the D.A.'s office."

"Yes, sir, this is Sergeant Murphy. I recognize your voice."

"Get McEwen and a couple of patrol cars to the Vann Hotel. Our witness in the Lashky case may be gone or dead. Paretti was talking, I heard shots, and then nothing, so send an ambulance too." Knox replaced the receiver, put on his shoes, pulled a .38 from a drawer, loaded it, and left.

...fumbling the receiver, Knox finally got it to his ear...

Five minutes later, Stephen flailed at the ringing phone next to the bed until he finally snagged the receiver.

"If that's you, Gil, I'm going to start pasting your photo on targets at the range."

"Do that Sergeant Thatcher and everyone's scores are going to go up."

"Murphy?" Thatcher looked at his clock. "What are you doing calling me at 1 am?"

"I'm pulling a double, so Ben Allen can go to the hospital and walk around in their waiting room while his wife gives birth to their first child."

Stephen shook his head to clear it, stuck the phone between his shoulder and ear, then reached for his pants.

"Since you didn't call me for that, Murphy, what's going on?"

"The D.A. lost Toller. Stanley Knox just called here."

"Where's Lt. McEwen?"

"That's why I'm calling you. He's not here, at home, or his two favorite bars."

Stephen suddenly felt a chill. Gil was never more than ten feet from a phone when on standby; half the time he slept on an Army surplus cot in the Plainclothes office. If Murphy couldn't reach him, the reason had to be bad.

"What else did Knox tell you?" He tucked the receiver under his chin and grabbed for his Argyles and Oxfords, careful not to trip over the long cord that let him bring the phone from the living room to the bedroom.

"Just that he spoke with Paretti, heard shots, and then nothing. I already sent two cars with Sergeant Evans in charge and called for an ambulance."

"Good work, Tom. I'll be at the hotel in ten minutes. Keep calling for McEwen until you get him."

"Will do, Sergeant Thatcher."

Stephen hung up the phone, then picked it up and dialed Angel.

"Wake up Ned!" Stephen shouted into the mouthpiece.

"Meet me just south of the Vann Hotel in an hour. Be ready for no more sleep until the sun goes down again."

Once Angel assured him he would be waiting, Stephen grabbed a fresh shirt from the closet along with his jacket but skipped the tie. He made it to the Vann Hotel, siren screaming, in nine minutes; athletic bag in the trunk.

As he pulled up, Stephen saw the ambulance crew loading Paretti into their wagon.

Where's his partner? He thought as he got out and ran into the hotel. A uniformed officer recognized him.

"Third floor Sergeant Thatcher. Room 327, at the end of the hall."

Stephen nodded and moved quickly up the stairs. Evans was waiting for him at the doorway. Paretti's partner was there, with Knox and the hotel doctor trying to bandage his head.

"What happened Evans?"

"From what Mr. Knox and I can get out of Klaffke there, they got a knock on the door less than two minutes after they discovered Toller was missing. Charlie went to see who it was," Evans pointed to a .38 on the floor. "Gun drawn like he was supposed to. According to him, the door nearly exploded, and he felt like someone hit him with a car." The uniformed Sergeant looked hard at Stephen. "We both know who that had to be; Lashky's pet gorilla."

Jerome "Golem" Kandel was the biggest goon in Great City; standing six foot five and weighing in at two-seventy-five, nearly all of it muscle and bone. Two years ago, it took five uniformed officers and a prowl car hitting him at 30mph to bring him down long enough to cuff him and take him to jail after almost beating to death the boyfriend of a girl he tried to pick up in a club.

Lashky thought it was funny to stick Kandel with the nickname since a real golem would have crushed the crime boss for his actions against his people, not protect him. One more reason why he was not welcome at either of the Temples in Great City.

"Yeah, Kandel got out of jail just four days ago." Stephen grimaced.

Hammond scripted and personally oversaw Kandel's parole hearing. The two have to be related.

"What happened next?"

"I can remember a little more now, Sergeant Thatcher." Stephen looked over to Charles Klaffke as the officer pushed away the doctor.

"What have you got Charlie?" He asked.

"Frank was reading and keeping an eye out until four when he was supposed to wake me up. It seemed like I just fell asleep when Frank was shaking me awake, saying that Vincent had escaped through the bathroom window."

"How long before Paretti called me?" Knox asked.

"Right after he woke me up." Klaffke rubbed his neck, wincing at the pain.

"I got up, put on my shoulder rig, and then my shoes." He looked at Stephen.

"I had just tied my laces when I heard the knock on the door. I ran to it, and then the door knocked on me."

"Did you see any faces?" Knox asked

"No, but the first guy filled the doorway. It has to be Kandel."

"Did you get off any shots?" Stephen asked.

"One. I shot at Kandel's legs, but I'm pretty sure I hit the guy behind him instead."

"Anything else?" Stephen questioned.

"I heard Frank shouting at them, and laughing because they missed Toller."

"Did he tell them that Toller ran off before they showed up?"

"No, he let them think he pushed Toller out of the window. Then something smacked me in the head and that was it until the Doc here woke me up."

"Did anything happen that would make Toller want to run?"

"No. Well, he had a little argument with his fiancée a few hours earlier, but I don't think it was anything. Maybe it was because Vincent called later than usual." Charlie tried to clear his head and nearly fell off the chair as he shook it.

"That's enough until you get him to a hospital and an x-ray to see if he's got a fractured skull." The hotel doctor interjected.

"Okay, Doc."

"What now, Sergeant?" Evans asked.

"Go downstairs, get on the radio and put the word out on the Golem and anyone else that belongs to Lashky, or Hammond for that matter. If dispatch tries to interrupt, use my name and Lieutenant McEwen's if you have to." Stephen grabbed Evans' arm as he began to leave.

"Don't say anything about Toller being gone yet. Then have a uniform downstairs run a message to Murphy. Tell him to send someone to go over to the fiancée's apartment; no uniform and no squad car, but make sure he's got his badge and his sidearm."

"You got it." Evans moved quickly out of the hotel room and down the stairs.

Stephen looked around the apartment and had just started on the bathroom window Toller crawled out of when Gil walked in.

"Evans gave me the short version and then went down the stairs so fast his shoes were smoking. Got anything else, Stephen?"

Before the younger officer could answer, Knox stepped in front of him.

"Where have you been McEwen? Toller runs off, and no one can find you!" Knox was ready to chew on Gil like he usually did to wife-beaters in court.

Gil looked like he'd been kicked by a mule, then shook it off and glared at the Assistant D.A.

"Murphy didn't have all the details. What happened?"

Knox told them about Paretti's phone call, heard the shots fired and ended it with him arriving just seconds ahead of Evans and the other officers.

"So what was so important Gil that you show up late?"

"I got a tip that the Moon Man was preparing to hit a gambling den, and

I went to check it out." Gil looked as embarrassed as a rookie officer who shows up for morning inspection with no bullets in his .38. "Turned out to be nothing."

"Now that we know where everybody was," Stephen jumped in before Knox could chew on Gil further. "We can figure out what's next."

"That's easy, Steve," Knox replied. "You and Gil go arrest Everett and then let me pistol whip him until he tells us what message he passed to Toller to tell him to run."

"I'll go along with the first half of that idea," Gil replied. "We've got to grab Everett so we can squeeze that ambulance chaser before Hammond realizes we have him." He pointed his chin at Stephen.

"Telling Evans not to mention Toller on the radio was smart. We can use that to make Everett think Paretti sent Toller somewhere safe and we still have him."

Knox looked at Gil sideways. "Hit Everett with it and see his reaction?"

"Are you still thinking Lashky's not involved?" Stephen asked.

"Still?" Asked Knox.

Stephen quickly related the conversation at the Thatcher dinner table yesterday.

Gil started to light a cigar, made a face, and then jammed it back in his coat pocket.

"I think someone got a conscience to save Toller, is trying to turn up the heat on 'Mercy', or maybe both. Whichever it is, the people involved just lit the fuse on that lunatic and we have to find Toller, or his corpse, before we start seeing people getting killed on street corners."

"Okay then, we need to get Everett before he goes to work and drag him in before he can squawk." Stephen said.

Knox nodded in agreement.

"You two grab him outside his front door, and I'll be waiting for you in an interrogation room at the precinct."

"Sounds good to me, Stan. We'll hand him over, just no pistol-whipping, okay?"

Knox rubbed his head and looked sheepish. "Yeah, about that …"

Gil chuckled. "We all say something stupid this early in the morning, Stan." He slapped him on the back. "You just have to remember not to say it in front of a reporter."

"Why don't you get over to the hospital to see about Paretti? Lt. McEwen and I can let you know if we get anything useful once we start shaking the trees," Stephen suggested.

"That's a good idea; thanks." Knox left without another word.

"Okay, tell me why you told a third set of eyes and hands to leave so soon?"

"That's easy Gil. Knox is a great lawyer, but he's got no training as an investigator or experience in reading crime scenes, just our reports. He'll just slow us down and maybe step on something important."

It also gets him out of the way before I have to ditch you so I can meet Angel.

"Good reasoning. You finish up the room and I'll start on the alley below the bathroom window.

"I got away from Gil too easy, this time." Stephen said as he settled the globe of the Moon Man over his head and secured the metal collar that held it in place.

"Do you think he caught on Boss?" Angel looked in the driver's mirror. "Is he tailing us now?"

Despite himself, the Great City vigilante looked behind them.

"No, he's got a bad case of lunar madness though. When I suggested splitting up to chase informants, he said 'yes' without a thought."

"Isn't that what we want; to keep McEwen off his game so he doesn't catch us?"

"I'm not so sure anymore Angel." The Moon Man related how Gil arrived late and why.

"He does sound a little screwy, but I don't think it's a problem we have to deal with yet."

"Let's hope you're right."

"Okay Boss; now let's go to Lashky's nearest gambling joint and start breaking jaws until something useful falls out on the floor."

"Ha! Hit the gas Angel!"

"All right, let him go."

CRASH! The thug flew through the air to land on a poker table, scattering money and players before bouncing off. At a nod from the Moon Man, Angel backed up out of sight and waited by the side door they had entered, so the attention was centered on the Lunar Avenger.

"Everyone pay attention! One lucky gambler or employee gets to keep his personal items when he leaves here tonight! That's the first person who can give me anything useful about where Lashky sent Vincent Toller."

That should stir up some trouble. Lashky knows that he doesn't have Toller, but he hasn't had time to get the word out to everyone.

One of the gamblers, though, didn't get the message. After trying the front door Angel had already locked, he turned to the Moon Man, full of liquid courage, put his hands up, and charged forward with a yell.

The vigilante hit him with a heavy left that dropped him to the floor and into Slumber Land instantly.

"Why don't you pick on someone else tonight? The cops already came by looking for you!" The manager of the club shouted at him.

"Your boss hadn't grabbed someone I need to talk to yet." The reflective globe bent forward for a moment.

"You've been running this club for Lashky almost three years now, Gordon Nance. You can probably tell me everything I need to know."

Nance didn't back up as the Moon Man approached, but he did breakout in a cold sweat. He knew how many minutes had to pass before reopening after a police raid, but the last gambling house the Moon Man attacked nearly burned to the ground.

"What I know about Toller is what I read in the papers. Anything that our boss, whoever he is, does about that is his business, not mine."

"Not good enough Gordon." The helmet let the Moon Man look around the room at all times with no one noticing. He let the two thugs move closer.

Angel's quiet, so there isn't anyone else moving around.

As both men suddenly charged the vigilante, he moved toward Nance, hitting him with a jab that took his air. As the man bent double, the Moon Man grabbed him by the shoulder and shoved him into the pair. Neither went down, but they both stopped cold, completely off-balance for a moment.

A backhand closed in a fist bloodied the mouth of the first one and knocked him on his backside. The second wisely backed up, but the Moon Man leaped over Nance to knock him down with a shoulder check the vigilante learned at Great City High as a sophomore.

"Enough!" Nance sat up and glared at the cloaked figure.

"No one's holding out on you Freak! We want you out of here, and the fastest way is to just tell you the truth." He rose to his feet and brushed himself off.

"If our boss grabbed Toller, then he's already had a taste of his mercy by now."

Inside the helmet, the Moon Man nodded.

He's right! I should have told him that Lashky was chasing Toller. Now the word's going to spread that Toller's dead and no one is going to talk.

After a few more, useless minutes, everyone had been walked out of the room after making a donation to Angel's charity bag. Wisely, he wore a full balaclava this time and thanked everyone with an Irish accent so bad, everyone knew he was faking it. Nance was the last to depart. As he left, he whispered two sentences.

"Look for guys that Lashky loaned out to Hammond. There's nothing to do for Toller, but something bad for everyone is about to happen."

Gordon dropped his wallet in the bag and then quickly left.

Mitchell Davis Hammond enjoyed being first into his firm's offices each morning. Unlike the other two senior partners in his firm, Mitchell turned down a corner office with his ascension to the fifth floor in the building. Instead, he took the three offices that lined the middle section of the floor, knocked out the middle walls, and redecorated it so that everyone who entered felt like they were approaching royalty.

Standing in front of the window, Hammond felt the sun on his face and reached up to carefully pat his famed and well-photographed, salt and pepper hair. As the sun continued to rise, the lawyer could almost feel it glowing like a pair of recently polished Florsheims.

"Mr. Hammond? Mr. Lashky is here for you."

"Excellent Miss Fitzpatrick! Send him in immediately." The lawyer grinned like a hungry wolf for just a moment, then turned to face Mercer Lashky just as the gangster walked in to his office.

The papers called Lashky 'The Gentleman Crime Boss'. Unlike most other gangsters, Mercer fit the description. He looked far more like Douglas Fairbanks than George Raft and dressed the part as well. His Brooks Brothers suits were tailored by Eli Grimbaldi, the same man who handled Hammond's wardrobe. His Egyptian cotton shirts were received in pieces and each one was assembled by Grimbaldi's apprentice only after new measurements were taken. The gloves he pulled off his hands cost as much as some automobiles.

His light, green eyes flashed brightly at every photographer and Lashky made certain he was only photographed with women from Great City's high society families. It was easy enough to accomplish with so many of those young women seeking the thrill of hanging on the arm of a known gangster.

Hammond walked quickly around his desk and warmly clasped his client's hands with his own.

"Thank you for coming in so quickly Mercer! As I said on the phone, this is the best thing that could have happened. With Toller running away from police custody, I'm certain Judge Harold will throw out the case. Even if he doesn't, I can't see him giving the police and the D.A. more than a week to find Toller and bring him home."

"If that rat accountant doesn't show, there's still those ledgers of his."

The lawyer shook his perfectly barbered head as they sat down at the large table in Hammond's office.

"Without Toller to explain his notes in person, it will be child's play for me to discredit them, you can be sure."

"Yeah, yeah, I know you can make those books look so cooked that the judge won't have any choice but to toss them out." Lashky sat down in the handmade, cushioned leather client chair.

"That's not why I'm here."

Hammond spread his arms wide.

"Well then, what else can I do for you today?"

The crime boss brushed off the top of his fedora with his gloves and then looked at the lawyer.

"Why was your boy Everett talking to Toller?"

Hammond dropped his arms, but still held his hands out in a welcoming manner.

"Basic intimidation, of course. The more often we hit Toller with these questions, the more likely he is to make an error that we can use. I'll remind you that it has already worked once."

"Yeah, I suppose you're right at that." A witness to Lashky committing an earlier assault on a now deceased bar owner, tripped himself up after a third questioning. Once the District Attorney's office dropped that charge, only the murder of the bar owner and the witness remained.

"That is what gave the judge enough distaste for this case so we could ask to see Toller almost at will."

"I still don't like it Mitchell!" Lashky slammed his hand on the table.

"The timing smells like a sardine factory! I had Kandel and a crew of good boys ready to put Toller in the bag. That would have handled him, and seen this done; permanently!"

"Maybe with the judge Mercer, but that would have put McEwen on your back for the rest of your life! With the Chief's son as his sidekick, to boot!"

Lashky leaned toward his lawyer and lowered his voice.

"That's the only reason I don't have your boy in one of my auto repair shops, hanging upside down from an engine hoist. If you don't eighty-six those ledgers, He's gonna need more bodywork than anyone in town can perform. I may not stop with him either. Understand?"

"Perfectly Mercer."

No matter how well you dress, Mercer, you're still the bastard son of a prostitute and one of the city's hoi polloi. Getting rid of you will line my pockets, but I'd do it for free after this little tête-à-tête!

"Good. Now let's compare notes Mitchell, and find this loser."

"An excellent idea."

He'll have to tell me everything if this is going to work. Hammond thought. *It will be child's play to keep his people running up dead ends and chasing their own tails.*

Before Lashky could continue, Hammond's personal secretary interrupted. Mona Fitzpatrick was the ideal-looking Irish lass from the picture shows and envisioned by writers like Samuel Beckett. Unknown to the rest of the law firm, Mona had recently added mistress to the personal duties of her job.

"I'm sorry to interrupt Mr. Hammond but we just received word that Duncan Everett was picked up by Lt. McEwen and Sgt. Thatcher."

Mercer looked ready to toss Hammond out of his fifth floor window.

"Looks like McEwen and his sidekick are on both of our backs, Mitchell."

Hammond merely shook his head with a vicious smile on his face.

"No Mercer, this is the beginning of the end for McEwen."

"So no luck with your snitches?" Gil looked at Stephen as the younger man stretched to try and stay awake.

"No. Even guys who have their ears all over Mercy's territory were surprised. A couple of them were even spooked by Mercy sending Kandel. A guy that recognizable is supposed to stay as far away from the police as possible."

Word spread faster than Angel and I could travel. I'd almost swear George Nance had a phone booth in his pocket.

"You know what that tells me Stephen?"

"That Lashky is so worried about Toller he's willing to take a big risk?"

"Exactly. That means a shake-up is coming and that's going to mean a war between the gangs." Gil shook his head in disgust.

That's near exactly what Nance said. Stephen suddenly felt like someone walked over his grave.

"We should have had someone watching the girl." Gil continued.

"You think now she was the one to tell Toller to run?"

The officer who checked at Anita's apartment woke the manager and then her roommate. Ellie Patterson was irritated at being woke until she got a look at Ned Pollard's bright green eyes and then couldn't be helpful enough. Anita left the apartment at 8pm, Ellie had said, to catch the overnight train to visit her Mother. She packed her bags that afternoon, long before Vincent called.

"It looks pretty likely, but you can be certain Hammond and Lashky know who she is and either one could have told her to warn off Toller or else."

"Could someone have warned them both so Anita wouldn't slow Toller as he ran?" Stephen asked.

"Now that's a real possibility." Gil nodded in appreciation. "Klaffke and Paretti talked about how Toller wanted to call her every night. That's more than just a knuckled-under boyfriend; he was looking for a message or passing one along."

Stephen looked over at Gil staring out of the passenger door window at the lobby entrance of Everett's apartment building. After a moment, he asked the question he was dreading to bring up.

"Who gave you the tip on the Moon Man?"

"I gave it to myself." McEwen's gaze never left the door, but his lips twitched into an embarrassed grin. "He's been falling into a pattern and I thought he was going to hit the joint again last night."

A pattern? I need to go over the last couple weeks with Angel and Sue again.

"You realize Knox isn't going to forget about this, right?"

"Yeah, that wasn't my best moment." Gil kept his eyes on the door as he finally lit his first cigar of the day.

"Maybe you ought to take that Father/Daughter vacation Sue has been after you about for the last two years."

"Set a wedding date, and we'll go exactly three months before then, Stephen." Gil grinned wide. "Not so much fun when the concrete shoe gets dropped on your foot, is it?"

"Getting married won't pull me away from the phone when I'm on call." Stephen retorted.

Before Gil could respond, Everett stepped through the door and began walking toward his car farther down the sidewalk. He suddenly stopped and

Gil kept his eyes on the door

stared at his car with its two, recently broken taillights.

"Hold that thought, kid!" Gil threw open the door and leaped out of the car.

"I'll have your badges for this!" The lawyer shouted as Gil pushed him into the unmarked squad car. "You know who my boss is; he'll launch another lawsuit against this department, and he'll win again!"

"Sure, he will." Gil replied as he climbed into the front seat and waved at Stephen to drive. He turned around and looked over the seat at Everett.

"Then a year later, two more judges will reduce the amount of money your boss won to only enough to cover his legal fees, leaving your law firm holding an empty bag, just like last time."

Everett glared at Gil and then looked out the window.

"The least you can do is tell me why you dragged me off the street."

"Someone tried to grab Vincent Toller last night. He got away to another safe house as two officers held off his kidnappers."

The junior lawyer stared back at Gil.

"That's impossible."

Stephen looked at the lawyer's image in the rearview mirror.

He's nervous. Everett didn't expect us to say we still have him, just like Gil thought.

"You sound like you were expecting me to say he's dead." Gil needled him.

Everett just ducked his head and refused to look up again.

"That's fine, shyster. I'd rather have this conversation in private anyway."

Knox pounded a fist on the table. "Toller was meek as a church mouse the entire time until you," he stabbed a finger in Everett's chest, "...came in and said something to make him run."

"Even if that were true, you and his fiancée should thank me. If it weren't for him running, Toller would be dead by now!"

"How are you so sure of that, Everett?" Stephen asked quietly.

"Do you think Lashky's boys wouldn't kill him right there in front of his guard detail?"

Gil grabbed the chair Everett was sitting in and slammed it to the wall. The lawyer fell on his backside, smacking the back of his head against the seat on his way down.

"That's funny counselor. When we brought you in, you acted like you didn't know anything about it. Now, you seem to know who showed up to try and grab Toller." Gil lifted Everett one handed to his feet. "If Lashky is as innocent as you claim, there's no reason for him to even look at Toller sideways, let alone waste a lot of time and effort trying to kill him."

The lawyer opened his mouth to respond. Before he could speak, the door of the interrogation room crashed open.

"Don't say another word, Duncan!"

Hammond strode into the interrogation room like he was approaching a jury and slammed both hands palm down onto the table with a loud smack. His salt and pepper hair was still perfectly in place and Hammond tried to pin both policemen with his best jury intimidation glare.

"We're leaving now!"

Stephen grinned as the well-coiffed and perfectly attired mouthpiece moved a finger between him and Gil like a metronome. "I defy you or your junior detective here to try and restrain us, McEwen!"

Gil did more than grin at the richly attired lawyer. He walked up to Hammond and blew smoke in his face.

"The boy is all yours Mitch. He's a really helpful young man."

The lawyer never lost his composure, but for just a moment, Stephen saw something a lot more dangerous appear in the man's eyes than the threat of lawsuits and writs.

Unlike his previous visit with Stanley Knox, Duncan Everett was quiet on his way out of the precinct. Even stranger was Hammond staying silent as well. As they entered Hammond's town car waiting outside, the older man gave Gil another dangerous look, pulled his door closed with a crash and ordered the driver to depart.

Before the town car pulled away, Stephen saw Angel getting out of his sedan and signaled him to stay put. McEwen knew they were acquaintances and had breakfast together now and then, but had no idea Dargan had any contact with the Moon Man.

"Gil, I'm going to tell Ned I'm too busy for breakfast today. It might be good to stay out here for a while anyway and see if Hammond has anyone watching us."

McEwen nodded. "You caught that look in his eyes too, huh? Okay then, see if anyone's hanging around that shouldn't. I'm going to get an unofficial APB on that Town Car and then see if Pollard is available to ask Anita's roommate if she remembers anything else." With that, Gil turned to go back into the precinct.

"Wait, Gil." McEwen looked over his shoulder at Stephen. "Hammond has always had it in for you, but this is different."

"I'm not sure, partner. The last time Hammond looked at me like that was when he couldn't break my testimony on the stand in the McReedy burglary trial three years ago, just before you made Sergeant." Gil started to light another cigar, then stopped. "I always got the feeling there was something personal about it, but I never could find out what it was." Before Stephen could ask another question, Gil turned away again and quickly entered the precinct.

Once McEwen was inside, Stephen signaled Angel to pull up.

"Follow that Town Car, Ned. We have a witness that just disappeared and …"

"You think that ambulance chaser Hammond had something to do with it."

Angel doesn't miss much. Stephen thought.

"Gil and I rattled the guy with him, Duncan Everett. He's a junior attorney at Hammond's firm and may be our only chance to find out what happened. Tell me tonight at my place what you find out."

"Sure thing, see you tonight." Angel pulled away to chase the large passenger car before it got out of sight.

Stephen watched him depart and then walked back into the precinct as the shouting started.

Moments earlier, Gil walked in and headed for Murphy at the front desk. Officially, he had no reason to order squad cars to follow Hammond. There was always the unofficial grapevine, however, once he got Murphy on the phone with his fellow desk sergeants.

Before he got halfway across the waiting area, Gil heard a sound right behind him and turned. As he did, he felt fire streak over his ribs.

With a yell, he spun fully around while taking a step forward and swung his arm wide. The knifeman behind him ducked, moved in to close the gap, and slash again at McEwen from left to right.

Gil pulled back in time, so the knife only made a shallow cut on his left forearm. As his attacker tried to step in for a closer try, he seized the man's left wrist, squeezing it to force the knife out of his grip.

"Gah! Leggo! For the love of God, let go!" Gil felt the bones in the knifeman's wrist crack in his hand like a dry stick, and let go as if he had just grabbed a lobster out of the boil pot barehanded. The stunned police lieutenant looked on as his attempted killer, holding his shattered wrist, collapsed to the precinct floor moaning for a doctor.

"I swear Mr. Hammond; I didn't tell them anything at all." The look of youthful confusion quickly left Everett's face. "Except for what you told me to tell them, of course."

"Very good Duncan." The lawyer looked benevolently at the junior member of his firm. "There was nothing you could know, so there was nothing to tell them."

Duncan thought over it all for a moment and then asked, "Why did you have me signal Toller and his girlfriend to run before Kandel got there? If Lashky isn't going to see the inside of a cell, why not just let his chief thug remove him?"

"That accountant has a wealth of knowledge about Lashky's operations that we can use once that criminal Neanderthal is dead and buried." Hammond held up a finger as he did in front of a jury.

"His disappearance also throws the attention of Lt. McEwen, Mr. Lashky, and Sgt. Thatcher away from our endeavors. Throwing in the girl's disappearance adds to the confusion as well.",

Hammond slapped his right hand on Everett's left arm.

"Although the junior Thatcher is also going to be busy looking for a new mentor soon."

Everett just nodded in response, then realized they were not driving to the law firm's offices.

"Is there a problem, Sir?"

"Certainly not my boy! I'm going to introduce you to a few friends of mine." Hammond wagged a finger at the other man. "Eliminating Lashky is the first action sponsored by a group of fellow concerned citizens, and we are always looking for young talent that knows what it takes to run a large city like ours."

Who am I meeting? The young man was about to ask his boss but decided to wait.

"Anticipation is good for you, Duncan." Hammond looked at him like he had read his mind. "Everyone should have a pleasant surprise in their life now and again."

I also need to find out if you let slip about Anita Newman to that damned McEwen.

"Will Mona be there Sir?" Everett pined for the striking redhead the way a schoolboy pined for his third grade teacher.

Ah the young! Hammond thought. *So easily fooled and controlled!*

"The dinner will be held at my home tomorrow evening. I will drop you at your residence to go out and buy an appropriate suit of clothes." Hammond handed Everett a business card.

"This isn't my tailor, of course, but Grimbaldi recommends him so don't even think about wearing that semi-tailored coat of rags from last year's Christmas party." Hammond paused for effect.

"To answer your question, yes. Miss Fitzpatrick will be there. Make certain to arrive promptly at seven o'clock."

Everett remembered Hammond's home from the Independence Day picnic. The place was incredible.

It's a perfect spot to tell Mona how I feel about her!

"Don't worry Mr. Hammond. I'll go there immediately. I won't embarrass you Sir."

"I'm sure you won't my boy. Just remember to go to the office after getting fitted for your new suit. You have a lot to do today and tomorrow with less time than usual thanks to McEwen, so get moving."

"You were lucky Gil. An inch or so lower, he would have missed the ribs and cut you a lot deeper; probably sliced into a kidney or stabbed you right in the liver." Harlan Pritchard checked his work on McEwen's ribs, moved his chair to the left, and began taking the bandage off Gil's arm.

"I don't feel lucky Doc. Hey!" McEwen jumped. "You're pulling the skin off with that."

"Stop complaining." Pritchard had retired from being an Army doctor in 1926 and spent the last ten years building up Saint Joseph into the best hospital in Great City. Whenever a police officer needed stitching up, Harlan liked to do it himself to keep his hands steady.

"I've sewn up at least half the police force, so try to hold still and not act like a society matron with gout." Pritchard's complete lack of a bedside manner irritated every parent who wanted him to go easy on their little precious, but it also made him a favorite with Great City's boys in blue. If Doc Pritchard chewed them out for complaining over a wound, they knew they were going to be fine.

"Fair enough, Doc. I'm more interested in how I put down Powell without hitting him." McEwen still looked like he had been caught beating a suspect with a phone book, something he wouldn't put up with unless there was a child in danger.

"I checked to see if Arthur Powell had records here; he does and his doctor is working this morning, so I asked him to come down and give you the details." Pritchard continued stitching up Gil's arm. "He should be here in a moment, but the short version is that Arthur Powell has cancer."

"How does that let me crush his wrist?"

"It's all through his bones, weakening them severely." Gil looked up as another doctor walked into the room.

"This is Doctor Thomas Bruce." Harlan continued stitching as the other physician began talking.

"Mr. Powell will be in a coffin before he gets that cast off his arm. I can't believe he'd waste what little time he's got left in prison." He looked at Gil quickly. "Not that I'm allowing him to be moved out of this hospital. If Arthur lasts more than two weeks, it will be a miracle."

"I won't try to argue Doc. The shape he's in, no warden would put him anywhere except the prison hospital, but I need to ask him a few questions."

"I put him under, and I'm keeping him that way for another twenty-four hours. You can ask him whatever you want after that."

As Gil started to ask the doctor another question, Stephen walked in.

"I just got off the phone with Emily down at records."

Emily Hill ran the Records Section for the Great City Police Department. She was one of the few Auxiliary Policewomen in the Department. It was a title with a badge, a uniform, an insultingly, tiny paycheck, and no real authority. Thanks to her unique filing system and incredible memory, however, every detective, and many of the uniformed officers, owed her a favor or two.

"You've never arrested this guy or any of his family that she can find."

"Then why did he try to stab me, especially in the precinct house?"

"I don't know Gil."

"You got his address?"

"Yes."

"I saw his wedding band, so let's go ask his wife as soon as the Doc here finishes up."

Pritchard snorted and leaned forward to look Gil in the eyes.

"If you tear open my embroidery within the next 24 hours Gil, I swear to you the next thread I put in you is going to be the fishing line I use for Walleyes. Then I'll tell Chief Thatcher to issue an order to keep you in bed for 24 hours."

As Angel followed Hammond, he started to think it was too easy. He continued with the Town Car after Everett got out and ran into his building with a smile on his face.

Is he that puffed up or has he got someone watching behind him to see who follows? He pounded a fist on the dash. *That's probably it.*

Once they arrived, Angel continued down the street past Hammond's home. There was a guard he saw in the rear view mirror, staring at him. The former boxer slowed down at the third house down the street and pulled up to the gate. Before the guard could order him off, Angel got out of the car and almost ran to the trunk.

He pulled out a box wrapped in brown paper and a clipboard, made a few notes, and then walked up to the guard as another car pulled into Hammond's driveway. From the view of the man at the foot of the driveway, it looked like Angel was just a private delivery man trying to drop off a package at a neighbor's home.

After a minute of trying to convince the gate guard to take the phony package, Angel got back into his sedan and drove past Hammond's home again. He had his cap pulled low over his face, and his arm in the frame of the open window. Glancing over to the lawyer's estate, he saw the driver standing in the open door, talking to the one at the gate. Angel instantly recognized the red-haired thug from the orphanage the day before. A second look and he recognized the dark-haired one he slammed into the rear door.

Angel accelerated past the gate and drove down the street, this time watching if anyone was following him. *Looks like I got something interesting to tell the Boss after all!*

As they walked up the stairs, Stephen and Gil heard a woman berating someone.

"Get out of here now! We're paid up and three months ahead! Arthur gave me the receipt, and I keep it on me all the time, so there's no use trying to lie about it or steal it when we're not here."

The red-faced building manager looked ready to blow as he turned from the door and approached the two detectives.

"What do you want?"

Gil took his badge from his pocket and shoved it in the man's face.

"Get lost before I call my brother in the Housing Authority and our cousin over at County Health."

"This is my building!" The manager snarled. "I'll call your boss and …"

His next words went out in a rush of air as Gil grabbed him by the shirtfront and slammed to the wall behind him and then threw the chubby, dark-haired man across the hallway.

"I said 'Get Lost'!"

The manager ran down two flights of stairs and slammed his apartment door as loud as possible.

Stephen knocked on the door the manager had just left.

"Great City Police Ma'am. Please open the door."

The woman who opened it was younger than they expected; there were just a few wrinkles on her fair skin and only a few strands of gray through her black hair. The Depression had left its mark, but she still had hope.

And now we're going to take it away. Stephen thought to himself.

"No one in my house has ever been in trouble with the Police. You must be looking for Arthur's good for nothing brother." Elsie Powell had started talking before she finished opening the door.

"No, Mrs. Powell. We're here to tell you that Arthur is in the hospital. He's in bad shape, and it's likely he won't leave under his own power." Gil's words were blunt, but his tone was almost sympathetic.

To Stephen's surprise, Mrs. Powell didn't argue further or look shocked. She stepped back and away from the door.

"Come inside; I'd rather not have my family's business spoken about in the hallway."

As the plainclothes officers entered the apartment, two boys looked out of a door on the right side of the hallway. Both were dark-haired and resembled their father.

"Keep your brother busy and quiet while I talk with the police officers Junior."

"Okay Ma." Arthur pulled his brother into the bedroom. "Come on Eddie, we'll get out your wood blocks and pretend they're a train on the way to Kansas City."

"Fine looking boys Mrs. Powell." Stephen told her.

"Thank you. Please sit down." She gestured to the sofa. It was clearly second-hand, but it was scrupulously clean with embroidered cloths on the arms. As he and Gil sat down, McEwen grimaced, but said nothing as Mrs. Powell continued.

"They're fifteen and eight. It's a good distance between ages. They don't fight over the same toys, but Eddie doesn't let Junior out of his sight some days."

Gil concisely explained what happened, including telling her where Arthur Senior was and how their doctor had him knocked out until tomorrow morning.

"Can I go and see him?"

"Of course." Stephen immediately answered.

Gil glared at him for just a moment.

"It's probably best to speak with Dr. Bruce before going down there. Hospitals aren't always the best place for kids." Mrs. Powell nodded in agreement.

"I knew Arthur had cancer, but he and the doctor told me it was just starting or whatever the medical term is." Gesturing with her hands, Mrs. Powell continued. "I knew he was sicker than he let on, but I never suspected this."

"How do you mean?" Stephen asked.

"He got a new job at the Kraus Department Store just last week as a floor watcher. You know, one of those men that keeps an eye out for pickpockets. He hadn't done much more than wearing sandwich boards or sweeping floors for the last year." A look of pride came to Anita's face.

"Our children never went hungry though. Arthur and I did, but not often." Then her face changed to grief just as quickly.

"This was supposed to be his first day. I should've known something was wrong when he left for work before I got up."

"What did he do this morning Mrs. Powell?" Gil asked.

"You see, he bought a new suit. Arthur said it was for the new job and part of his advance, but he left it in the closet. New shoes too!"

"We heard you tell the landlord you're caught up and paid ahead on the rent, Mrs. Powell." Stephen prodded gently. "How much did Arthur bring home?"

"It was $300, and he left the rest of it here. Arthur said last night he was only taking enough for the bus, lunch, and a cup of coffee at an automat." She looked at him. "There's $85 left, do I have to give that back now?"

"No, Ma'am." Stephen jumped in before Gil could ask for it. "There's no need for that."

After a few more minutes, they left Mrs. Powell to her grief. Stephen looked to Gil as they walked out of the apartment building.

"He had it all planned out Gil. Right down to the suit to be buried in."

"Powell probably thought the other cops would shoot him dead right there after he knifed me."

"I guess that's why he didn't wear the suit to kill you."

Gil turned and put his hand in Stephen's chest hard enough to stop and push him back a step. He grimaced again.

"You know we needed to take that cash. The next time you don't follow procedure and put me on the spot like that, I'll take it anyway and put you back in uniform before the end of the shift. Sue can give me all the grief she wants, but it won't do you any good. Got it?"

"Yes, Gil."

"Good, now let's go do something useful and find out who paid Arthur Powell to take a run at me." Gil reached back to his ribs and pulled back his hand with blood on his fingers.

"Right after Doc Pritchard stitches me back up again." McEwen pulled his handkerchief out of his coat pocket and wiped his hand.

"If I'd known that was going to happen, I'd have thrown fatty down the stairs for good measure."

Knox nearly tore the door off the Plainclothes Office as he barreled inside. The Assistant DA was disheveled, with his hair a mess.

"I finally figured out how Everett got his message to Toller! It was the order of the questions!" He stopped talking and looked around the office.

"Where's McEwen?"

"He's in the hospital resting, trying to convince Doc Pritchard to let him out and that new Nurse of his to take care of him at home."

"Hospital? What happened?"

Stephen looked at Knox in amazement then related what happened.

"How much do you think Lashky paid Powell to do it?"

"Gil doesn't think it was Lashky. He's got his money on Hammond." Stephen related the conversation with Mrs. Powell.

"I see Gil's point. Hammond's slicker than any other lawyer in town, so no one has been able to hang anything on him." Knox shook his head.

"Gil has sure tried to, that's for certain. Even when Powell wakes up, I'll bet he got the money and orders through someone that had no ties that we can find to Hammond." Stephen leaned back in his chair.

"Now what's this about Everett changing how he asked questions?"

"He switched the third and fourth questions he asked." Knox replied.

"I finally got a handle on it after I read my typed up notes from the previous depositions. The question switch was the only difference I could find."

"Did he do it before?"

"Yes, two weeks ago. Everett switched the fourth and fifth questions."

"Did anything happen then?"

"Not that I can tell, but I asked Paretti and Klaffke to look over their notes

"Hospital? What happened?"

for the week after that and see if anything stands out."

Stephen remembered Klaffke's words that night.

"See if they wrote down the time of Toller's calls. Charlie said something about him calling Anita later than normal the night he ran."

"Good catch Stephen. If that is the case though, it means Anita is in on it."

Knox groaned and rubbed his hands over his head, mussing up his hair further.

"That means we're looking for two people who ran with a reason, a plan, and using Hammond's resources."

"Sue! How's your father?" Angel waved at the young woman halfway up the stairs to Stephen's apartment. The attack on Gil McEwen had made the evening edition.

"He's grumpy, irritable, and has decided to sleep at the precinct house when Doctor Pritchard lets him go tomorrow. I even threatened to elope with Stephen if he didn't come home." She paused on the second-floor landing to let Dargan catch up.

"I'm surprised he's resting at all. When Stephen called me from the hospital and told me what happened, I figured your old man would be out busting up every crooked operation trying to find out who put the finger on him."

Once they entered the apartment, Stephen filled them both in on the details about Powell and taking Gil back to the hospital. Once he finished, Dargan laid out everything that happened.

"Are you sure about this, Ned?"

"Definitely. There were two of the three guys I ran off from the orphanage."

Stephen rubbed his chin thoughtfully.

"I think your dark-haired thug is Dennis Burkhart. The thing is, he's supposed to be a wheelman for Lashky."

"This is getting a little too coincidental Stephen," Sue spoke up. "Angel runs off what turns out to be a crook that works for Lashky, and then the next day, a witness against Lashky disappears shortly after one of Hammond's junior ambulance chasers talks to him."

"Yeah, and minutes before Lashky's men tried to grab him." Stephen concurred.

"It always smells like fish around guys like Lashky," Angel wrinkled his nose. "But this is a different stink."

"I think you're right, Angel. Hammond has always walked on both sides of the law, but he's got something planned here I don't think Lashky is aware of."

"I agree Boss, but how does the orphanage fit into it?"

"Maybe Hammond has plans for the property," Sue replied.

"You may be right about that Sue. Now Angel and I …"

"Time to go out in the moonlight, darling?" Sue looked at Steve and then nodded toward the well-used canvas bag. "Or are you really going to the gym for once?"

"Come on now, Sue." Angel grinned at her. "You know he's only going to say something sly like 'I promise you, dear, I'll get a good workout' and then wink or something like that." Both of the Moon Man's trusted associates laughed.

"Real funny you two. I ought to try and put you on the radio after Edgar Bergen and Charlie McCarthy." Stephen rapped his knuckles on the table between them. "Now pay attention, I've got an idea on how to look for Toller while playing on what those thugs were arguing about in the warehouse a couple of nights ago."

"You mean if you're a Martian or a ghost?" Dargan asked.

"That's it, Ned. I read through Wells' novel again, and here's my idea for after we grab Burkhart."

"I'll bet that skinny redhead is with him when we do."

This don't feel right. Burkhart slowly woke to realize he was tied to a chair. When he realized that the ropes felt sticky, cold, and then hot; but still smooth underneath, he began getting nervous. Then, a deep hum began vibrating the floor and walls around him as the air made him feel as if he could throw up.

"Fergus! Where are you?" As he struggled to get free, the thug squinted against the foul air and tried to looked around.

Where am I? How did we get pulled out of Danson's Bar?

Unknown to Burkhart, finding him was not a problem for Angel. All he had to do was go into the cheapest dive bar he could find to ask about three guys with the injuries he handed out. Luck was with him, and Dennis and Red were already there. Two sawbucks later and the bartender was happy to drug them and even help Angel haul them out.

That's why you always pay your bar tab on the first of the month. Angel thought to himself as he threw Red into the back of a car for the second time that week.

It smells like a tar pit in here. The dark-haired thug tried to look around again, but his eyes watered too much and he could barely move his head in any direction.

"Dennis Burkhart!"

He tried futilely to turn his head again, only to realize that the same, sticky rope was holding it in place. This one was warmer than the others holding him to the chair, however.

"We need to talk about your new employer. You've driven for Lashky for two years, but it now looks like Hammond has been pulling your strings for some time." The Lunar Avenger leaned in closer to Burkhart.

"In case you weren't paying attention, Lashky has been a favorite source of cash, among other things, for me the last few months. Now, his lawyer seems to be getting involved." The globed vigilante tapped a finger on Burkhart's forehead. The thug felt his skin pull away from his skull before the finger let it go, snapping back in place.

"That's fine, but I need to know what his plans are for Lashky's operations. You will tell me everything you know, starting with why he ordered you to kidnap Irene Vandergilt."

"You got it all wrong! We weren't putting that rich broad in a bag; we were there to make her pull her support from the orphanage."

"Why? What use is the orphanage to Hammond?"

"I don't know. We were just loaned out."

The Moon Man leaned in closer, signaling to Angel.

"Lashky might loan you out to Hammond, he'd never allow anyone else to do it."

The sticky binding around Burkhart's head started growing hot.

"That's the truth! Don't burn me!"

After a few moments of increasing heat, the Moon Man moved behind Burkhart and signaled to Angel. Dargan quickly changed the water that flowed to the hoses that held him tight from the hot water tap to a bathtub filled with cold water and a broken up block of ice. In less than a minute, Burkhart began to shiver.

"Very well Dennis. Now, let's talk about what happened last night. Where did Hammond send Vincent Toller?"

"I don't know; I wasn't the one that …" Burkhart stopped suddenly. Before the Moon Man could signal him, Angel had already turned the flow of hot water back on.

"Now is not the time to hold something back, Dennis."

Burkhart started pulling at the chair as the heat around his head and neck increased. He twisted even harder, but it only rubbed his skin raw. The burning increased, but he remained silent.

"Perhaps, you need more incentive." The Moon Man moved toward Dennis' red-haired partner.

"What do you mean?"

The man under the Argus glass gave a long low hiss.

"I'm hungry. Your friend is a little past his prime, but still edible."

Moving to block Dennis' view with his body, the Moon Man drew a staple remover from his cloak. Carefully avoiding anything vital, he punctured the skin over James' spine; just enough to make the blood well up.

"What are you doing to Fergus?"

At another signal, Angel flipped the switch on a battery hooked to wires in the unconscious man's socks. Fergus jumped as if he could feel the bite of it. The jerking movement made the blood on his neck splatter on the Argus glass and the black cloak.

Dennis could see the blood drip down the globe. As he looked down, the front of the cloak suddenly moved toward him, as if something was trying to get out, to feed on him.

Oh God! It's not Vandergilt he wants! He feeds on those kids!

"Ahhhhhhh!" Burkhart pulled at his bindings so hard; he would have pulled the chair over if Angel hadn't nailed it to the floor.

"It was Dobbins! I took Toller and the girl to Sonny Dobbins! We changed cars and drivers in case anyone saw us leave the hotel or the girl's apartment! He took them to Carl Hopkins at the docks! Now stop it! Stop eatin' him!"

"The wax coated ropes and rubber hoses covered in tar and kerosene worked perfectly, especially with hot water running through them. I think Burkhart confessed to every crime he's ever committed in Great City, Angel."

"At least now we know how Toller got out of Great City."

In response, the Moon Man removed his helmet. Stephen nodded in agreement as he began placing his costume into the gym bag.

"Not to mention the information we have on Hammond now. He only recently got his hooks into Burkhart, but Dennis admitted that Hammond started co-opting men from Lashky's organization at least six months ago." Angel shook his head slightly.

"I think it's been longer than that, Boss."

"I do too, Angel. For Hammond to move like this, he had to have started recruiting men for a year at least. Especially for a hard case like Carl Hopkins."

The former boxer looked thoughtful for a moment. "Isn't he one of Lashky's main enforcers down on the docks?"

"That's right Angel. He's tough enough even Gil has a grudging respect for the man. If we're going to get anything out of him, we'll need a plan before we grab him tomorrow night. Tar covered, hot water hoses are not going to break him."

"I was thinking on that as you were working on Burkhart, Boss. A guy we put away last year can help us."

Tuesday, September 11th

"Your honor, you have to give us more time!"

"I protest as well Judge Harold." Hammond sneered at Stanley Knox. "There is no reason to give the District Attorney's office any time at all! The witness changed his mind and decided to stop lying about my client; a simple businessman that …"

Harold banged on his gavel until the block underneath began to bounce.

"Both of you shut up!" He pointed at Hammond. "I've seen those ledgers, so save your 'simple businessman' palaver for a jury!" He turned to Stanley Knox.

"I think a week is more than fair. Your witness decided to run off, and before you say anything about Jerome Kandel, Toller crawled out of that window before there was even a knock at the door!" He slammed the gavel down hard one more time.

"Right now, neither of you look competent enough to order a tuna fish sandwich at a lunch counter, let alone appear in my court!"

Both lawyers opened their mouths to argue, but Judge Harold waved them to silence.

"The trial begins in one week, with or without Toller. The D.A.'s office can present his evidence, of which there is still enough by my determination, so don't ask for another evidentiary hearing Hammond. If you cannot convince a jury, Mr. Knox, learn how to nail shut a window next time!"

"I thank your honor for his decision." Hammond jumped in first and then turned to sneer again at Knox.

"I'm sure we'll have Toller back here in seven days your Honor. Thank you." Stanley ignored Hammond completely as he left the courtroom.

"That's all Judge Harold gave us, Chief Thatcher. The people of Great City have seven days to find Toller and present him to the court. If he's not here by then, I won't give you a plug nickel that we'll ever find him."

"Then we have to find him before Lashky's people." Peter Thatcher looked at Knox from the other side of the younger man's desk. "Stanley, I have a request. You won't like it, though."

"I get it, Chief. There's a chance someone in my office put out where we had stashed Toller so you want me to keep information on the case as restricted as possible."

"We'll do the same on our end, of course." Chief Thatcher grimaced and shook his head.

"We found officers on Lashky's payroll last year, and I hate to admit it, but we probably didn't find them all."

"Since Paretti and Klaffke are out," Knox told the elder Thatcher, "That leaves only two other guys I trust completely. Quentin Lerner and Ted Mitschke are out of the 14th; been with my office for a full year."

"Good. Have them get in touch with Stephen. Gil stays on bed rest for at least 24 hours, as far as I'm concerned. My son can coordinate with your investigators and any detectives he trusts to run down the most likely trails for Toller."

"I thought I would know more people here Sir. You said I'd be surprised by the membership."

Everett looked around the room with a mix of excitement and panic. It was only after they arrived that Hammond explained the meeting would be after dinner and Everett should relax in the library until he was called.

"A number of our supporters try to remain out of the public eye as much as possible." Hammond clapped the younger man lightly on the shoulder. "There are quite a few people here tonight that live very modestly, but are some of the wealthiest men and women on the Eastern Seaboard; even after the Crash."

"I understand Sir. They don't want to wind up in some do-gooder's column, getting excoriated for refusing to give away their wealth to people who don't know what to do with it."

Hammond nodded appreciatively.

"An excellent breakdown of the situation Duncan."

"They also try to avoid law enforcement when possible. After all, while you may know and even appreciate that the policeman on the corner is taking protection money from the business owners on his beat, you never know who he is talking to when passing up part of his take."

"Knowing what we do about Lashky, Sir, I can certainly understand that."

Hammond looked ahead and signaled that he was heading to a knot of well-dressed bankers and one politician.

"Come with me, I'm going to formally introduce you to Deputy Mayor Davis and a few of our silent partners that he works with to direct our city council along the right path."

Three hours, and a meal, dessert, and several, single malt whiskeys later, Mona appeared as a vision in blue before Duncan.

"Good evening gentlemen. May I pull Mr. Everett away for a few moments? He looks like he could use some fresh air."

"Ha Ha! Lead away Miss Fitzpatrick! I think we've bent the young man's ear enough for now." Hammond motioned for Everett to get up.

As the two departed, one of the bankers immediately went back to business.

"Are you certain that Toller's girlfriend will finish her task?"

"Oh yes, in addition to being well-paid for her trouble, we also have the incriminating evidence that Anita poisoned her last fiancé. Well, three of them to be exact, but the police will only be able to prove the last one with what we give them."

"Remuneration and blackmail. An excellent combination of incentives Mitchell; well done!"

Despite having the focus of his dreams on his arm, Duncan still felt slightly irritated at being pulled away. Once they reached a small table for two, carefully placed by Hammond, he voiced his exasperation.

"There was no need to rescue me Mona. It was an interesting conversation."

"Then consider this you rescuing me. I was having a very boring conversation and needed a reason to escape. I looked up and there you were!"

Duncan's irritation melted away like a snowball on a floor furnace.

"I can't imagine any conversation you're a part of being a boring one, Mona."

This should be easier than Hammond suggested. The dark-haired woman decided.

I can't imagine there isn't a thing he won't tell me.

"You're a dear, but I want to hear about your run-in with the police. Did they give you the third degree like on the radio?"

"Oh no Mona! McEwen and Thatcher had no idea what was really going on. If Mr. Hammond hadn't arrived when he did, I would have had them jumping over the table like a high school track team."

Mona leaned in and placed both hands on Duncan's.

"Tell me more Duncan. It sounds so exciting!"

"You should have seen their faces when I told them that they and Toller's fiancé should thank me if I really did warn Vincent off! I thought Knox was going to …"

"What do you mean Duncan? Did you mention Anita Newman to those wretched officers?"

"Her name never left my lips dear Mona."

"Really?" She carefully raised one delicate eyebrow. "Dear Mona is it?"

"Of course!" Duncan finally got out after several stumbles. "I would do anything for you Mona my darling."

"Well, I'll have to think of something for you to do then, won't I?" She caressed Duncan's right cheek with her left hand and gave him a barely there kiss on his left cheek.

"For right now, though, let's return to the party and toast your escape!"

As they left the table, Mona considered Duncan's slip.

A half-truth at best! She thought. *I should have expected it from that schoolboy. He probably made some foolish crack about Newman, thinking the police are too thick to catch it. I'll keep this from Hammond and then maybe I can still use Duncan against that arrogant pig when Lashky decides to deal with him.*

Carl Hopkins woke to a world that looked like he was held underwater, but with flames somehow burning everywhere. The sights around him looked like a pulp magazine he once swiped off a newsstand. The lurid cover promised murder with exotic mermaids swimming around, awaiting his every command.

The nightmare that moved into his line of sight was no mermaid though. At first, the thug could not understand anything; he only noticed the rising heat and that he was sweating through his coat in the coldest autumn he could remember.

As the Moon Man watched Hopkins try to orient himself, he thought back to the adventure where he struggled with the same gas. The phony psychic used it to pull information from his clients and then feed it back to them as messages from beyond. He also used it to learn safe combinations and safety deposit box numbers his companions used to rob the wealth of Great City.

He nearly did me in as well. It was Sue and her pearl-handled automatic that gave me the distraction to get away.

Hopkins got to his knees, then the Lunar Avenger stepped around from behind him and said only one word.

"Boo!"

Hopkins, one of the toughest longshoremen to work the Great City docks, screamed like a child who sneaked into a showing of Dracula and tried to curl up in a ball, sure that Lugosi was coming after him. He pulled so hard on the ropes securing his hands behind his back that he nearly dislocated his left shoulder.

"Greetings from beyond Carl. Your mother and sister send their regards, and are looking forward to seeing you soon."

That brought Hopkins' head off the floor. He couldn't look at the macabre vigilante directly, only sideways and just for a second. Smoke seemed to be rising from beneath his cloak.

"Soon?"

"Yes, Carl, soon. It's not even your criminal life that kills you; it's one of the unhappy husbands of the wives you've corrupted."

In addition to smuggling, Carl specialized in a thin slice of loansharking. Giving money to women trying to keep their homes together while their husbands looked for work. Nearly all of them fell behind, and Carl always demanded 'personal favors' as payment.

"I'll stop! I'll tear up their IOUs! Whatever you want!" Carl started hyperventilating and nearly passed out until the Moon Man picked him up and dunked his head into a washtub full of ice water.

The cold water shocked Carl enough to wake him up but left him in the grip of the gas. After a minute of naming everyone he could think of who worked for Lashky, the Moon Man interrupted him with a slap to the face.

"Now that you know what awaits you, Carl, I'll give you the chance to avoid that fate for a few more days at least."

"Anything!"

"I know you took delivery of Vincent Toller and his woman, where did you send them?"

"I don't know; they had four places to jump ship before the *Captain's Lady* unloads at Havana." Carl provided the locations and started to calm down. "Why do you want him so badly?"

"Hammond may own his life, but my master owns Toller's soul, and it is time for Vincent to pay up."

At that, Hopkins finally gave in to the effects of the gas and passed out, dreaming of lakes of fire.

Stephen removed the Moon Man's globe with a coughing fit. The smoke he used to help frighten Hopkins had leeched a little underneath the collar to irritate his nose and throat.

"Hopkins was the key Angel! Did you get the names of those harbors where that ship was stopping before it went to Cuba?"

"Yeah, Boss." Angel looked at the list he wrote. "Keystone, Akelton, Brunswick, and Miami."

"Keystone is too close and I don't think they went to Cuba, probably not even to Miami. Toller and Anita had to have gotten off the ship at Brunswick or Akelton."

"I got friends in both cities, Boss. You know the one in Akelton."

"Yeah, nice fellow for a guy that used to be a second-story man."

Angel nodded in agreement, then spoke up. "So we're done looking."

"Once you call your friends, we'll give it a couple of days. In the meanwhile, I still want to try a different dodge on a name Hopkins give us that I recognized; Eli Shoemaker. Toller said several times that he was a friend and wanted the D.A. to stay away from him if he could."

Angel grinned at the comment.

"I guess it makes sense that a bookkeeper and a numbers guy like Shoemaker would have something to talk about over a beer. How are you going to handle him, Boss?"

"Not just me, Angel. All four of us."

Stephen chuckled as his partner looked confused, trying to do the math.

Wednesday, September 12th

Eli Shoemaker had run illegal lotteries for nearly three years, and worked as a runner for Frankie 'Friar' Tuckman before that. Not that Frankie wanted to retire, but once Eli broke every finger on his right hand, he decided that living with his sister and her family in South Carolina was a good idea. For Eli, that was gratitude for all that Friar had done for him. Tuckman was a lefty.

I can't believe that freak hung me off the roof for half an hour.

Shoemaker was still shaking from the cold as the Moon Man tied him to the radiator, and left the empty office for the room next to it.

Sullivan's Island is looking pretty safe and quiet now. I wonder if Frankie's still holding a grudge.

The Lunar Avenger slammed the door, jostling the recently broken transom hinge, opening it almost halfway. After a few moments, Eli could hear the vigilante dialing a number and then one end of a conversation.

"I'm telling you, Max; after this job, I'm not putting this helmet back on until

He was still shaking from the cold as the Moon Man tied him to the radiator

the boss starts cutting us in on a bigger piece of the action. The four of us are doing almost all the work now, and he barely even leaves his apartment now."

Four of them? Shoemaker listened closer.

"No way am I saying we get rid of him! The guy's made us a fortune over the last two years; what I'm reminding you of is that you and me are the last of the original crew except for him."

I'll be hanged! We have been killing him. Their boss just keeps finding replacements!

"Naw! This guy doesn't know anything about Toller. I think that Hopkins guy just put us on him to stop me from crushing his toes with a hammer."

"I'll murder Hopkins for that," Eli muttered to himself. "But first I'll drop that fishbowl in a bag." He pushed himself up against the radiator, trying not to burn his hands.

"You still out there? I got something else for you if you swear to cut me loose!"

"Do you think we can trust him, Boss?"

"I don't know Angel. Lashky dropped out of sight a few hours before Toller vanished. If Shoemaker was telling the truth about his boss getting ready to run if he didn't get the bookkeeper, then this is the only place we know for certain where he'll be before he leaves Great City. We have to be there tomorrow and in place before he arrives."

"Letting him loose ain't sitting right with me. This seems like one of those times we need to trick McEwen into getting involved. At least he could keep Shoemaker locked up long enough to let us get set up and spring a trap."

"With McEwen still on bed rest on orders from Chief Thatcher, there's always the chance that Shoemaker could convince someone to let him near a phone and tip off Lashky. Being surrounded by a lot of cops might even give him more courage, and then we'll never find his boss."

"OK, then; I'll back your play. I just hope you scared him enough to run like he swore he was going to."

"I hope so Angel. The only alternative was to kill him. We'll let Sue know tomorrow morning and get everything ready."

"Can we trust Shoemaker, Edward?"

"Yes Mr. Lashky. If you'll recall, Eli was the first who alerted us to Hammond's scheme three months ago."

Edward Schulman was a highly educated man with an immense talent for planning, and a desire to never earn an honest dollar in his life. After he planned a bank robbery to coincide with an armored car heist that divided the police response and both teams got away with the cash, Lashky made him a senior lieutenant.

"What about Eli being friends with Toller, and why did he say it was going to be Monday?"

"Not a problem, Boss. After he explained what he knew of Hammond's scheme, I had to stop Eli from running out and killing the accountant himself as a show of loyalty to you." Edward shook his head. "As for Monday, he wanted to give us time to prepare a good response and he figured it would be suspicious to suddenly give that freak what he wanted in a few hours."

"Okay then, we'll take care of this fishbowl-wearing vigilante, get rid of Hammond at the same time, and make it look like they killed each other."

"What about Toller?"

"As long as he's out of town, he's low on my list. Now get hold of Mona and tell her it's time to put her boss in a bag." Lashky allowed a vicious, little smile spread across his face.

"Let's make certain of it, Edward. Have two of your people go out now to rig up a few surprise greetings just in case."

"An excellent idea Mr. Lashky. I know just who to send out there."

"Make certain to give Shoemaker an appropriate bonus for picking the Stevens Office building. It's surrounded by other abandoned buildings and perfect for getting rid of Mitchell and his favorite errand boy."

"Of course Mr. Lashky."

Thursday, September 13th

"So that's everyone involved, huh?"

"Everyone who was there Mr. Lashky. I got the feeling there are a lot more politicians and high society types looking to make you the first step in getting the whole pie." Mona almost purred as she betrayed her boss.

"Ha! So the silver spoon set wants to get in the gutter themselves? I don't think so."

"Remember how many of your people Hammond has brought into his organization. There are probably other members of his little group doing the same thing to the other gangs in Great City."

"That's a good point to consider Mr. Lashky." Schulman stepped into the conversation.

"Yeah, I suppose you're both right about that." Lashky looked thoughtful for a moment and then over to Mona.

"See if you can turn Hammond's favorite errand boy to our side of things."

"Duncan might play along, but I'm not certain I have him wrapped around my finger quite as well as Hammond."

"Give it a try, Mona. If he turns you down, try to get him to give you a day so you can run away from everything."

"I'm not sure Mr. Lashky."

"I don't care if you're not sure, give it a try and if he won't go along, call us once he leaves your apartment. I'll have Schulman here handle him quietly."

Mona just waved her hand.

"Quiet or loud is not my concern. He's just another one of those men that thinks he can save me from a life of whatever he believes I'm in." Mona snorted her disdain.

"The price is always the same for do-gooders like that, however."

Cold as ice and always looking out for her own angle. I'd keep her myself if I didn't think she'd knife me soon as she had enough cash.

"Then you should enjoy getting rid of him if he doesn't play ball Mona."

"You can tell me who I have to sleep with Mr. Lashky, but don't even try to tell me what or what not to enjoy."

Oh yeah, Lashky thought. *I'd have that knife in my guts real quick!*

"Let's talk about something I will enjoy; when are you getting rid of Hammond?"

"It's funny you ask, because Edward and I just spoke about that yesterday."

"Oh? Well let's hear it!" Mona leaned forward with a genuine smile on her face.

"Is everything okay Mercer?"

"It's all perfect darling; just like you." At that, the young blonde squealed just a bit and threw her arms around Mercy's neck. Carolyn Beatrix Scott was as in love with Lashky as he was with her family's standing in high society. A champion tennis player in college, the athletic young woman was the opposite in personality to Mona Fitzpatrick.

"I'm so glad. Now let me show you what I have planned for the menu after the judge throws out that silly, little case against you."

The beautiful blonde grabbed the crime boss' manicured hand with her own carefully lacquered nails and pulled him toward the plans laid out on her family's dining room table.

Coming out here is a risk, but it's worth it to keep my foot in the door with the Scotts.

Mercer had planned for years to marry into Great City's high society for the protection and to expand his operations. To his surprise, the well-connected Scott family had not once tried to run him off.

"This party will be the biggest event on the social calendar Mercer, everything is carefully laid and …" She turned back to Lashky and crossed her arms over her green, silk dress.

"It would also be an exceptional time to announce other important events, especially ones that require a question, an answer, and a particular piece of jewelry."

Lashky threw his head back and laughed out loud. He kept it just low enough, however, to avoid a glare from Theroux, the butler.

"Why do I get the feeling someday I'm going to walk into this home to find a minister, flowers, your parents, and twenty complete strangers."

"Oh don't be silly. I'll make certain the groomsmen are my friends that you have already met."

I suppose that wouldn't be so bad, not all of her friends are stiffs. At least I don't have to worry about her father being involved with Hammond. The old man even seems to have warmed up to me recently.

According to Mona, none of the Scott family was involved in with the lawyer's group. In fact, the name never came up in any report about Hammond or his co-conspirators.

Friday, September 14th

"Please Mona! You have to understand that I owe Mr. Hammond everything!"

Is he going to turn on me now? Mona thought.

"Then I suppose you'll have to turn me over to Hammond now?" The stunning redhead added a careful tremble to her voice as she pulled her shoulders back slightly, stretching her silk blouse tight across her chest as she leaned forward.

"Please Duncan. At least give me a few days to decide where it is safe for me to run to before I leave."

It wasn't needed, as the infatuated young man had already decided to help her leave.

"Of course darling! I know everywhere Hammond has contacts, so I can make certain there is no one who will be looking for you."

"But what if Hammond pressures you? What if he … tortures you?" Mona feigned breathlessness as she stopped speaking.

Everett looked thoughtful for a moment and then smiled brightly.

"I'll give you a list of the cities where I know the firm has no interests. That way you can choose where you want to go and I can't tell anyone what I don't know."

That was quick! The only problem is if he decides to tell Hammond after all.

As Everett continued to talk about how else he could help her, Mona began to think about how Mercer was going to get rid of him along with her, soon-to-be, ex-employer.

"It's been well over twenty-four hours and Doc Pritchard let me go."

"I was there Dad. He also said to go someplace quiet and rest for a couple of days."

Gil held up an open hand and lowered his fingers one-by-one.

"See there Sue; not a sound. It's quiet as a church in here."

Before she could respond, a quick knock was launched against the door to Gil's office.

"Come in!" Gil shouted, then grinned slyly at Sue.

In walked two of the shortest police officers Gil had ever known in his career. The height requirement for Great City Police was 5' 5", but McEwen was certain Quentin Lerner and Theodore Mitschke were both at least an inch under that. He never looked into it since both men were as tough as Benny Lynch, one of Gil's favorite flyweight boxers.

"Mr. Knox sends his regards Lieutenant McEwen." Lerner spoke up first. His blonde hair was so light that it almost looked white. Mitschke merely nodded, a shock of black hair falling across his forehead.

"Good to see you both." He nodded toward Sue. "This is my daughter, she helped me get settled in and is just heading home." Gil looked pointedly at her.

Sue's glare was just as hard as her father's, but she knew she wasn't going to win this one; yet.

"I'll check in with you later Dad." She nodded at the two officers. "Nice meeting you both, just make sure he follows doctor's orders."

As the door closed behind her, she heard Mitschke ask, "Are you sick Lieutenant?"

That'll teach him to try and dismiss me like he does Stephen!

Monday, September 17th

"Are you quite certain we have to do this now Mona? It seems to me that finding a pro bono office should be done in the daylight with a photographer in tow." Hammond was irritated, not really about looking at office space, but at having Duncan Everett along, preventing him from running his hands over the lovely woman.

"Now think about it Mitchell. Wouldn't the effect be better by showing a law office already prepared to serve the underprivileged of Great City? Reporters just love that kind of thing." Mona looked at Everett. "Isn't that right Duncan?"

"Oh, yes, Miss Fitzpatrick." The young lawyer nodded until his neck hurt. "It's great publicity for the firm Mr. Hammond, and a way to stay on top of issues we don't want to see walk into the uptown offices."

Hammond pretended to throw his hands up in surrender and then looked out the window as his Town Car sped toward their destination.

"I do hate to see bums and indigent families fill our foyer, especially in the summer months. Fine then, a visit to Cannell Avenue and then to Chez Grand Plaisir for a very late dinner."

"Sue, is Stephen there? I need to reach him now!"

"He's on the way here Dad. What's wrong?" Sue had just started preparing dinner for her and Stephen at his apartment.

"Why are you in such a hurry if you're at home resting on Chief Thatcher's orders?!"

Gil was not healing as quickly as Doc Pritchard wanted and went directly to Thatcher to put him back on bed rest. That lasted until Lerner and Mitschke arrived with a second-hand rumor about Lashky raising his head to deal with a legal problem.

"Chew on me later Sue. We got an anonymous call about two of Lashky's people sniffing around on Cannell Avenue near the docks. This may be where Mercy is hiding out before trying to leave town. Tell Stephen this may be our last chance to bring him in."

"Where is it Dad? Stephen should be here any moment and I can send him there before he can get out of the car."

"That's my girl! The address is 1941, just before Cannell crosses with J Street. It used to be the accounting offices for the Stevens department store. I'm coming down there nice and quiet with Knox's people right behind me to avoid spooking him. Once Stephen arrives, we should be able to wrap up everyone there."

"Don't worry Dad. I'll make sure he gets there." *If he's not there already.* Sue thought as she put down the phone.

The young woman immediately went into Stephen's bedroom and removed a waist holster from the closet. After quickly looping it onto her belt, she pulled a .32 automatic, identical to her own, from the built-in gun cabinet, then loaded and holstered it. Sue then inserted rounds into a spare magazine, threw that in her purse, grabbed her hat and coat, and ran for her car.

Stephen's changing cars with Angel at the gym again, maybe I can get to Cannell before them.

As he approached the office building, the Moon Man felt the hair on the back of his neck rise.

Angel was right; we should have waited or turned this over to Gil.

The Lunar Avenger checked his .45 one more time, and made sure the extra magazines were in his front pants pockets. His flashlight and a sap each hung off a snap loop on opposite sides of his belt.

I also should have gotten a new shoulder rig and one cloak instead of two after that arsonist nearly did me in last year. No wonder the pulps always make their heroes rich playboys.

Hammond roared in disbelief at Lashky turning the tables on him. The worst part of it was when Mona pulled a pistol from her purse and leveled it at him with a steady hand.

"Sorry Mitchell. Lashky pays a lot better than you ever did. He also didn't fill that nice apartment you kept me in with the cheapest furniture you could find."

Kandel sprung the trap seconds after Hammond walked through the door, shoving the lawyer hard enough to land on his dignity and then lifting Everett by his shirt front and tossing him to land next to his boss.

"When I get out of this, Mona, I'm going to squeeze the life out of you myself and then throw you in a ditch."

"Ha! This isn't a jury to talk your way around Mitchell. It's your execution squad." Mona looked over to Kandel.

"I'm leaving now. Mercy never said anything about having to watch."

The big thug nodded at her.

"Go ahead Miss Fitzpatrick. We'll take care of 'em both."

As she left, Mona caught a movement out of the corner of her eye. She saw the Moon Man too late to do anything, but saw another man moving toward the other end of the brick building.

Those two could ruin everything!

She ducked behind the Town Car, waited until he passed her, counted three, and then stood up with the snub-nose .32 in her purse out and ready.

"Hold still runt." She thumbed back the hammer and then shouted, "You've got company, Kandel!"

"Easy lady." Angel held up both hands to show they were empty.

"No pistol? What were you going to do, try and talk Lashky's golem into giving up?"

"He doesn't need a gun." Before Mona could turn her head, Sue grabbed her by the collar and put the muzzle of her automatic against the other woman's neck. "He's got me."

"No good honey. I can still shoot the little… Ow!" Angel snatched the gun from her hand, nearly breaking her finger in the trigger guard.

"Thanks for the souvenir beautiful!"

"Go help him." Sue told Angel. He turned and ran toward the building, now alive with gunfire.

"So now what? You going to shoot me?"

"I ought to," Sue replied, "but helping get rid of Hammond might be considered a public service. Turn slowly toward the street, start walking without looking behind you, and then go back to whatever corner you came from."

As Mona departed, Sue took a deep breath and ran inside.

"You've got company Kandel!"

At the shout, Jerome punched Everett in the stomach to empty his lungs, then grabbed him by the throat and squeezed.

"Get Hammond out the back! Mr. Lashky wants to finish him all by his lonesome when he gets here!"

As Kandel spoke, Everett tried for the big thug's face. His fingers just barely brushed the Golem's chin, and Kandel laughed as he pretended to try and bite them.

"You should've been a better boyfriend, then maybe Mona would have kept you out of this."

CRACK! Lightning flashed behind Kandel's eyes. He turned around to see the Moon Man pour the lead shot out of the sap in his hand. One of the leather seams had split on Kandel's skull, making it useless. The big man barely noticed the blood running down his neck from the cut on the back of his head.

The globed vigilante stepped forward and landed a solid shot on the big man's chin. The second blow finally made Kandel drop the nearly unconscious Everett, but now the Golem gave all of his attention to the Moon Man.

"I'm going to crack you like an egg!" Kandel shouted.

Now I know why they had to hit him with a prowl car!

The thug moved faster than most big men, but he was still slow compared to the Lunar Avenger, who stayed out of his range, and stepped in only when he had a chance to split an eyebrow or something equally damaging.

As Angel ran toward the fight, the Moon Man saw him and nodded the Argus globe to the left. "Hammond was dragged out that way!"

His partner nodded, and took off after the lawyer. He saw Sue running in the same direction a moment later and almost called out to her. The split-second distraction was enough to let the Golem get close enough to land a haymaker that twisted the helmet around, bending the collar so it no longer held the globe firmly in place.

Spinning and falling with the blow, the Moon Man launched an elbow while almost on his knees. He hit high, to the side and above Kandel's left knee, bending it backwards and sideways, sending the big man hopping backwards until he tripped. With a roar of pain, he crashed partially through a wall of sheetrock, pinning his injured leg underneath him.

Stay down long enough for me to catch my breath! The Moon Man thought.

Kandel was also breathing harder as he pulled himself out of the wall, so he changed tactics before he blew himself out. Instead of trying to land a crushing blow, the big man feinted until he got a hand in the cloak. Before the Moon

Man could slip himself out of it, Kandel hit him in the chest until he started sagging on his feet. Then, the big man began swinging the Moon Man around like a cruel child with a small dog on a leash.

"It's like playing 'round the world with a busted yo-yo!" Kandel smashed the Lunar Avenger into one side of the hallway, and then the other. As they neared the far end, the Golem let go of the cloak. Once he fell to the ground, Kandel kicked the Moon Man in the ribs hard enough to slide him toward the doorway of the last room. The vigilante didn't register the shots being fired elsewhere.

Too far! The Golem realized too late. Just before the vigilante slid into a doorway, the massive crook turned and dived quickly to right.

BOOM! The Moon Man felt like the legendary John Henry had struck him on the top of the head with his hammer. As his hearing slowly returned, he also realized he could feel a breeze inside the helmet.

What hit me? Police training and two years as Great City's Robin Hood kept him moving. Once he pushed himself out of the doorway and farther into the abandoned office, the Moon Man felt the top of his helmet. As he suspected, the Argus glass was spider-webbed, and pieces fell away as he touched them.

Kandel! He leaned back toward the doorway and looked out to see the huge thug stumbling down the long hallway, hands grabbing his left side, and leaving a trail of blood behind him.

As he turned his head again, the Lunar Avenger could hear something rolling around inside the remains of the helmet. Carefully unlatching the collar, he set the two halves down on the floor next to him and picked up the small, round piece of metal that fell out.

"Shotgun pellet," Stephen muttered to himself. "If I hadn't already been on the ground before I hit the tripwire, that blast would have cut me in half."

He pulled off the collar next and looked it over. The deflector plate that directed his breath down past the collar was undamaged, but the steel rim itself would need work. Looking around, he wrapped it and the two shattered halves in a drop cloth and hid them inside a hole in one of the office walls. As an afterthought, he stuffed the cloak inside it as well.

I'll come back for you later! Then he ran back into the hallway and retrieved his .45.

BANG! BANG!

Angel! Sue! Stephen checked his automatic then moved quickly toward the sound of gunfire.

Angel ran all out, catching up to Hammond and the two thugs. He put the first one down with a crushing right to the kidney and then smashed the jaw of the second with a left, sending him to dreamland. As he turned back, Hammond picked up the Webley dropped by the first thug and swung it toward his rescuer. The former boxer quickly dove behind an abandoned wood desk as Hammond fired twice. One of the heavy rounds buried itself through the top and into the drawer beneath it.

Rushing in behind Angel, Sue fired a moment later, her .32 tearing a hole in Hammond's coat and suit, leaving a burning gash across his right side. The lawyer yelled in pain and frustration, then fired two shots back in Sue's direction without seeing her.

"I don't hear anyone identifying themselves as a police officer, so I'm guessing you're tied in with our resident, Selene inspired, vigilante."

"What's your point shyster?" Angel called.

"The longer we wait here, the more likely the police show. You'll be arrested, while I, as an officer of the court, will immediately press charges. If you let me go now, I'll walk away."

"Too bad for you I just got here Hammond!" Stephen called out. "All three of you are under arrest, so come out with your hands up!"

Hammond bent down and set the Webley on the floor.

"I was merely defending myself after a kidnapping attempt. Now if you don't mind, I'll wait outside while you arrest these criminals." Hammond sneered, opened the back door, and then walked out.

Fine. Stephen thought. *I'll arrest you anyway once Sue and Angel get out of here.*

BOOM! BOOM!

The bursts from a shotgun filled the air. Hammond jerked twice like a marionette handled by an angry five-year-old, then fell to the ground, dead as his dreams of power. As Thatcher took a step forward and saw what the second blast did to the lawyer's lower jaw, he heard Lashky's voice called out to him and a breach close.

"I heard you in there, Thatcher, so I'm leaving now before any more cops get here! Stay put Junior and you don't have to join Hammond tonight! We'll catch up another time!"

"Too late for that, Lashky!"

Stephen stepped over Hammond's corpse to see Gil walk up and stop about fifteen feet away. More than close enough for the Winchester 1879 in his arms or the .45 now tucked in his belt. Lerner and Mitschke were both off to his right.

"Glad to see you finally got here Stephen!"

"I could say the same for you, Lieutenant!"

Sue fired, her .32 tearing a hole in his coat and suit

"I know you and Junior there won't take a bribe McEwen." He squinted at Gil as the night continued to darken. In another twenty minutes the sun would completely set and getting away would be far easier.

I hope my next lawyer is as good as Hammond, otherwise I don't have a snowball's chance at getting out of this one.

"So, how do you want to do this?"

"Pretty simple. Once I stop talking, you drop that Baker double-barrel you're so fond of behind you, and walk over to me. Wait too long and I open up." Gil took a deep breath and closed his mouth.

Lashky put the Baker on the ground and sighed heavily.

"Put 'em down boys." He looked at McEwen with regret.

"Much as I'd like to throw down with you Lieutenant, I'm not dying for that shyster; at least not today."

Gil walked up to and then behind the crime boss. Lerner and Mitschke cuffed the two gunmen after they laid down their own weapons.

"Looks like you're getting smarter in your old age Mercy."

"At least I knew who was coming after me and why. You're not going to be so lucky."

Gil looked at Lashky and then turned his head toward Stephen.

"Use my radio to call for a wagon and an ambulance for Everett. The car's around front."

"On my way Gil!"

Stephen ran back into the building where Sue and Angel waited.

"Angel, grab my helmet and cloak from the little office at this end of the hallway. It's all in a hole in the wall. Put them in the car and be careful not to cut yourself. The globe is broken."

Sue gasped as Angel went to collect the shattered helmet and cloak.

"What happened Stephen?"

"We'll talk about it tonight at the apartment. I have to get an ambulance now."

"Good, I have a lot to tell you as well." Sue grinned at him and then moved quickly through the building and out the front.

How does she move that quietly on concrete in those heels?

Stephen heard Duncan Everett groan and start to wake up. He quickly grabbed the junior lawyer by his collar and began dragging him to Gil's car.

I hope Gil still has that extra pair of handcuffs in his glove box. Stephen laughed to himself as he saw Dargan pull away.

I left mine in Angel's car.

As they waited for Stephen to return, Gil looked at Lashky and then gave him a shake.

"Okay Mercy, drop the other shoe."

"You ought to thank me McEwen."

"For what? An easy arrest for once?"

"For getting Hammond off your back. You never did figure out why he had it in for you, did you?"

"I broke his streak of wins with the McReedy convictions."

"Yeah, but what you and your pals never caught on to was that McReedy was Hammond's cousin."

"No chance Lashky. The D.A. ran a background check on McReedy when they figured out his method was the same for heists up and down the coast."

"Yeah, I helped Hammond with McReedy's papers awhile back. Even got him a Social Security number as a Christmas present back in '35. It was a lot easier then since a couple million people were trying to get one before the New Year."

"Any other skeletons in the shyster's closet I should know about?"

Lashky shook his head and smiled.

"That's the only one you get for free McEwen. Don't worry though, at least two of them are going to come looking for you and Junior now that Hammond doesn't have a hand on their leashes."

"Why would he stop someone from getting rid of me?"

"So he could pay a guy sick as Powell to do it for him without any of it coming back to him. If your fellow badge boys didn't shoot him on the spot, Hammond promised Powell he'd pay up the rent for his family for a year."

Then why did Powell pay three months in advance anyway? Gil asked himself.

"I got a hard time believing you Mercy."

"No reason not to cooperate McEwen. Hammond was responsible for everything I've been accused of for the last three years."

"Good luck pushing that."

"You think Knox or your own Chief won't play ball if it means closing twenty open cases or so?"

"No matter what, I've still got you for murder."

"Maybe so McEwen. I'll take my chances in court."

Saturday, September 15th

Vandergilt sounded a little odd on the phone. I wonder if she's still having problems with those two idiots.

Angel drove through the Vandergilt gates and parked in the same spot. Henry greeted and escorted him inside again. Irene looked disappointed as she spoke.

"Please understand Mr. Dargan, I understand why you run around at night with that vigilante. I even acknowledge the need for such activities at this time."

Irene leaned forward across the table and placed her chin in her hands.

"What I cannot risk, however, is that one of your partner's enemies discovers who you are and then takes revenge on my employees or the people I have dedicated my life to helping."

"I understand Miss Vandergilt. Can I make a suggestion?"

"Of course."

"Make Julie the director of the orphanage. Except maybe for Althea and yourself, there's no else better to help the kids in this city than her."

"That's an easy suggestion to take Mr. Dargan."

"What can I say; even us delivery boys have a good idea now and then."

"Ha!"

After a few minutes of small talk, Angel said thank you and departed. Once he closed the door behind him, Irene's gate guard entered from a side door.

"Mr. Dargan took it well, Ma'am."

"Yes he did. I can admire what he and his companion are doing, but I can't have it tied to any of our shelters or kitchens."

"Of course not Ma'am. Do you think any of the dirty money has worked its way into your operations?"

"If it did, then it's doing more for the poor of Great City than ever before. I'll keep taking it for now."

Alton Terry grimaced inside, but smiled and nodded in agreement. After Irene dismissed him, the guard returned to his post at the gate.

Following that runt paid off! I got him off the property, but it's too bad I couldn't convince Miss Irene to break off all ties with him. I can't believe she still wants to use the money Dargan and that freak steal from crooks.

Alton settled in his chair and checked the log to see the grocery delivery hadn't left yet.

Maybe I can send word anonymously to Dalton about him. She would probably cut him off immediately and badger Miss Irene to do the same.

Mollified for the moment, Alton moved back slightly and put his feet up on the desk.

Eventually, she'll see that I'm the only one she can trust.

"Hello Mr. Everett." Davis stepped up to Duncan's bed, but made no effort to shake his hand or otherwise touch him.

"Good afternoon Deputy Mayor Davis."

"How are you feeling young man?"

"Not good Sir. With Mr. Hammond gone, I'm out of a job and, in a few months, out of my apartment."

"Don't worry about that, there is always room for a sharp lawyer at another law firm. Especially when the new, senior partners already know how loyal he is to the 'concerns' of Great City."

Duncan sighed in relief.

"I'm really glad to hear that Sir." He plucked at his blanket for a moment, then looked up.

"Has anyone heard from Mona?"

"No Duncan, she seems to have disappeared from Great City."

"Oh. Well, I guess I can't blame her. This is no place for a girl like her."

Girl?! Davis thought. *Good grief, the young idiot is still infatuated even after she basically threw him to Kandel.*

"You may be right young man, but we need to talk about you, specifically what you intend to do with the knowledge you gained from Hammond and our Concern for the future."

"There's no need to worry about that Deputy Mayor Davis." Duncan somehow managed to straighten up even while lying on the bed. "This whole incident has taught me that Mr. Hammond was right about the need to guide Great City into an even greater future."

"Then we can count on you?" Davis quickly stuck out his hand, right above Everett's own. The young lawyer immediately grabbed it.

"When the alternative is men like Lashky and that madman in the globe helmet that chases him down? You absolutely can count on me."

Sunday, September 16th

A day later, Angel received a telegram from down the coast which he gave to Stephen.

"Met your acquaintances. More through official channels. Suspect engagement off." It was signed 'Tommy'.

"We'll have to find a way to thank him Angel. That little trip last year to help out Mr. Pedlar certainly paid off."

Official word came to Chief Thatcher that evening from his counterpart in Akelton City. Vincent Toller and Anita Evans were discovered in a motel after gunfire was reported by the owner. Police broke in to discover Anita trying to kill Vincent by shooting through the thin, bathroom door. She had already hit him once, leaving Toller with an ankle to match his broken heart.

Newman was to be held over for trial in Akelton City while Toller would be escorted back to Great City on Monday morning with a cast, a cane, and a barely used engagement ring in his pocket. A quick call to Knox was met with joy, but Judge Harold merely snorted after being informed.

"Who cares about your witness right now? I have to wait for Lashky to get out of the hospital and then allow him to find a new lawyer and get ready for a new trial! Toller can show up after New Year's Eve now if he wants, because I may even have to rule his testimony and his ledgers inadmissible because of his and his fiancée's connection to Hammond!"

Chief Thatcher politely thanked the judge for his time and hung up the phone. Then he patted a patched hole in his kitchen wall. It had been five years since he punched the hole, breaking three knuckles on the frame behind the drywall.

"At least he was seen shooting Hammond, or I'd be sitting across from Lashky and the Mayor at the City Hall Christmas charity dinner."

"You've got a visitor Lashky. Let's go."

Mercy walked into the visitor's room and froze in place until the guard gave him a hard shove forward. Before he could recover from his shock, Weatherbee Scott got to the point.

"Let's skip the pleasantries Mercer. Have a seat." Carolyn's father gestured to the chair opposite his own.

"You're wondering if me being here means all of your plans to enter high society are as dead as your chances of getting out of here before you're old enough for FDR's communist safety net."

After a moment of staring at Lashky, Scott continued.

"It won't be soon, but you will be getting out in a reasonable amount of time. Six months later, you and Carolyn will have a wedding so lavish that every flake of this city's upper crust will have to attend or be ostracized."

"How?"

"A family history lesson first. While I had money of my own, it was made by me, making me unsuitable, or so I thought, for Carolyn's mother. That is until Evelyn's father called me to his club for dinner and drinks. Turns out the old man had a lot of secrets that would make a few matrons of high society faint dead away."

"I'm confused Sir; Elgar McIntosh was the tallest pillar in Great City."

"Oh he certainly was; great contributor to the poor, etc. He, along with his father and brother, also owned several successful pirates raiding ships off Cuba for over five years. It was in that fifth year, they raided what turned out to be a gold transport for a minor European duchy that all but vanished in the Great War."

"How does this involve you and I?"

"A secret relating to something even stranger than the gold was rearing its ugly head, and Elgar asked me to cut it off for him. Which I did of course." Scott leaned forward. "Literally."

"You see Mercer, hanging on to old money is difficult, but keeping this type of old money out of sight is far more problematic. That is why I never argued against Carolyn seeing you. I had to know that you are the type of man she, and the family, needs to keep everything going like it should."

"I have to admit I'm shocked Sir. Does Carolyn know the family history?"

Scott leaned back with a knowing smile.

"Only a few jokes about grandpa being a local version of Blackbeard. If you think this is shocking, wait until I show you the gold; Son."

EPILOGUE

Arthur Powell Senior got his miracle, plus a day. Unlike Hammond's funeral a week earlier, this was an open casket ceremony. Arthur was buried in his new suit and shoes, just like he wanted. The people who came wanted to say farewell to a friend and neighbor. At Hammond's service, two members of the funeral home staff had to stop a former client from opening the casket to drive a stake into the corpse's heart to "make sure the bloodsucker doesn't come back".

Surprisingly, Mrs. Powell asked Stephen and Gil to be two of her husband's pall bearers. When questioned, she said that Lieutenant McEwen and Sergeant Thatcher had been politer to her and visited Arthur in the hospital more than most of his so-called friends and especially his no-good brother. Even with that endorsement, after the ceremony, Stephen and Gil stood away from the gravesite, near the cars.

"What about the money we know Hammond paid Arthur, Gil?"

McEwen shook his head. "Let the widow keep it, Stephen. Even though her church picked up the bill for the funeral, she'll need it. It won't do anyone any good if we take it now. The money will just sit in evidence for a few years and then get turned over to the City Hall general fund to pay off more shysters like Hammond."

Stephen was hoping to get the money back to the widow somehow, but Gil just leaving it with her stunned him for a moment.

"How do we work that?"

"Did you put anything about it in your notebook?"

"Yes, but what about the final report Gil?"

"I already wrote it. I stated that Arthur Powell was paid enough to catch up on the rent, pay ahead three months, buy a new suit and shoes, a switchblade, and had just enough left for the bus, and a sandwich with a cup of coffee from an automat. That's the only money we can account for, and the only person who could've said otherwise, Lashky took care of for us." He looked Stephen in the eye.

"Too bad you accidentally threw out the page with the dollar amount in the garbage tonight."

As the Powell family walked by Gil and Steve, Elsie smiled and nodded at them, but kept walking to the waiting family car. Arthur Junior carried himself with more dignity now than many men twice his age. As they approached the waiting vehicle, he stopped his Mother with a touch on her elbow.

"Take Eddie and go on to the car, Ma; I want to talk to those police officers."

Gil and Steve braced themselves for threats or whatever, but Arthur Junior gave them a surprise.

"How do I become a police officer?"

"Why do you ask that?" Stephen asked.

"My Dad told me everything about him slashing Lieutenant McEwen. You took care of Hammond for him, but there are a lot more out there, just like him and Lashky."

Gil looked him up and down.

"Okay kid. Let's see what you've got." He raised four fingers.

"You have to be eighteen, good grades in school, stay out of trouble, and a written recommendation from your High School Principal," Gil told him and lowered his hand. "Then you've got to make it through the Academy."

The young man nodded and looked at them both. "I can do that. Our neighbor across the hall already watches Eddie after school, but Ma needs help with the bills even with her going back to work."

Gil interrupted him. "Come by our station house next week, and we'll find you work after school. You can help out your Mother, and put a dollar or two away for your future while getting a leg up on the other cadets in a few years."

Arthur Junior nodded again, spun on his heel, and left to join his family.

"Looks like you picked up a stray of your own Gil."

"No, Stephen, I got a chance to pay back his Father."

"How do you figure?"

"Arthur Powell had me cold; he could have slipped that knife right into a kidney before I knew he was standing there. Instead, he missed, gave me a scratch that bled real pretty for everyone to see, put another one on my arm, and then I dropped him."

"So you think Hammond had someone there watching to make sure he earned his pay?"

"Expensive shyster like that; of course, he did."

"Miss Vandergilt tells me that you and Althea both recommended me for the job, Ned."

"It was an easy choice Julie. There's no one better to run Vandergilt's new kid's home than you."

"Especially after you turned her down."

"I would have been the wrong choice, and Vandergilt would have seen that the first time she caught me making two kids get in the ring to settle their problems."

Julie smiled at the picture of Ned acting as referee.

"You're probably right, but that is not the main reason I wanted to meet you in my new office." The young woman paused a moment, then continued. "Regardless, I'm uncomfortable working closely with someone I'm romantically involved with." Julie stopped, letting the comment hang in the air.

"So that's why we're here, not to congratulate you on a new job, but to give me the brush-off?"

"Not entirely Ned, as I just said."

"If I had taken the job, and you were my right-hand, would you still break it off?"

Julie flushed with embarrassment and irritation.

"It's different for a woman Ned. A female boss has to be twice everything a male is, especially virtuous."

Angel thought for a moment and then nodded slowly.

"I suppose you're right, I don't believe Althea Dalton's had a date since the Crash."

"I would like it if you came by like you do with Althea though. You're a good example of what the boys need to be and what the girls should expect out of any man in their lives."

"I can do that." Julie brightened at the agreement.

"Good! Now, Irene already gave me a petty cash fund to get things rolling. How about if I treat you to lunch this time?"

"Okay by me. I'll even order dessert for once."

That Evening

"Are you sure about this, Boss?"

"Yes, Angel. It'll be a while before the new Argus helmet arrives. Once we start up again, no more calling Gil after every job."

"I guess that's a good idea if a guy like McEwen ain't where he was supposed to be."

"Yeah, Gil's getting obsessed, so from now on it's an anonymous call to whichever precinct house is closest to where we hit a gambling den or smash some other racket."

"I guess that's why you didn't order the new globe under his name like you did the first one?"

Stephen smiled and then grimaced at the memory of Gil finding out the helmet of the Moon Man had been supposedly shipped to him. His response was unprintable in any newspaper.

"I'm glad your friend in Akelton was okay with being the receiving address for us."

"He said once we pick it up; we're jake for last year Boss. McEwen can't squeeze anyone down there even if the glass company reveals the address again."

"Tell him we still owe him a favor. It's not like I can make my helmet."

"Good thing you ordered a spare this time to go with it."

"Change of subject Ned. How are you and Julie doing?"

After Angel told him what happened earlier, Stephen let out a whistle. "That's pretty rough pal. You okay?"

"It makes sense boss. Julie needs to be at her best if she's going to give those kids a chance." Angel blew out some air.

"What's got me worried like a dog's favorite bone is that Irene Vandergilt figured out I'm working with you." Angel relayed to Stephen the conversation earlier.

"You're just full of good news tonight Ned. Any guesses on how she did it?"

"I don't know yet, but I'll find out. I guess I wasn't as careful as I thought."

"Don't blame yourself; we've been busier than normal what with grabbing so many thugs off the streets. It was probably some waiter or dishwasher stealing a smoke in an alley we crashed through and happened to recognized you."

Two weeks later, the other crime bosses had divided up most of Lashky's territory. Everyone agreed that final control would only be established after he went to prison for life or landed on death row. Control of the docks and warehouses were split between two Italian factions, and a gang run by one of Great City's premiere Irish criminal families took over his gambling operations. Loansharking, prostitution and the rest were still being traded off between the new bosses.

No one knew where Edward Schulman and Jerome Kandel had disappeared. Everyone agreed that if they came back, then it was only smart to offer them a reasonable piece of the city. If that didn't work, then they would start shooting and not stop until they all ran out of ammunition.

"Shine those lights in every corner! Check every rafter and support overhead."

"Come on, Bernie! We've been over everywhere twice already."

"We're gonna do it four times if you give me any more lip, Stanley."

The rest of the goons grumbled but continued looking.

It's a different warehouse, but some of the same crooks. The Moon Man realized from his hidden location. A few minutes later, Bernie spoke up.

"OK, all of you can stop now. There's no way that freak is going to jump us this time."

"Are you sure he jumped you last time? That's a big leap for anyone."

"That's why I'm telling you, he ain't even human!"

Hello Lenny! Hope you like the cell they give you this time!

"Knock that off Lenny. Did you hear about Hopkins and Shoemaker?"

"You mean them almost killing each other?" Lenny asked. "Yeah, Eli nearly had him cold. If he'd put that shot a little higher, then Hopkins would have dropped at his feet instead of having time to grab the gun and start beating him with it."

"Knock off the chatter and pay attention!" Bernie interrupted. "Just because he's not here, doesn't mean he won't show up!"

"He hasn't been around in almost a month. I think the Golem actually got rid of that freak this time."

"If Eli is right, there's at least three other guys ready to take his place."

THWACK!

As the warehouse went dark, the Moon Man slipped out the false back of the rigged crate Angel paid two friends to set up earlier that evening. Lenny turned around just in time to see the helmet, almost glowing from the moonlight coming in through the windows, moving toward him, but not the fist that laid him out.

THE END

LUNACY AND THE LUNAR AVENGER

Maybe, perhaps lunacy is a harsh word. A little crazy has to apply though. About three months into it, this tale was at eight thousand words with the ending in sight. Then, my computer crashed so hard, it was actually hot to the touch for several minutes. Instead of putting the Moon Man aside for greener pastures, I went back to the drawing board with several pages of hand-written notes in my grubby fist. In case anyone asks, rebuilding a lost tale is much harder than starting a new one.

On to Stephen and his group of friends and partners however! Unlike a few of the more extreme vigilantes, Stephen Thatcher did not put on his helmet after someone close to him died. That makes it harder on the writer who now has to do more than just mention the dead in passing, have the character shout "Vengeance is mine!" and then shoot up a warehouse full of goons. Our hero got into this to help people, not necessarily to punish them. I hope that came across with this story.

One thing I noticed in a number of old pulp tales with the weirder heroes, was the fact that the lower-level goons seemed to spend more time than their bosses trying to figure out what their vigilante was, and not just assuming it was an ordinary guy in a mask, hood, or helmet. I can't recall where a pulp character took advantage of that, except for the Shadow of course, so the idea stayed in my head, and wouldn't leave, even after the digital meltdown. Spiritualists were still around then and conspiracy theories were all over the FDR administration. I thought that throwing a few aliens in the mix would make for an interesting sub-plot. Hope you like it.

Next up for Stephen and his fellow crime busters? I originally had the Vandergilt and Evans families in a subplot, but finally realized that it was taking away too much oxygen from the Moon Man. I cut it out for the next tale, so we'll see Great City's high society at its best and worst in a future story with the Lunar Avenger. Enjoy!

Kevin Findley—was raised by a kindly couple in a small town in Kansas. Unfortunately, he lost his red cape as a child, so he put on a different blue suit after college and flew around the world as an officer in the U.S. Air Force, defending Truth, Justice, and The American Way.

In his twenty years as a Logistics Specialist, he traveled to such interesting places as Germany, Japan, and the United Kingdom, among others. Surprisingly, he is still allowed in all of those countries. He retired at the rank of Major.

Kevin has been writing for Airship 27 for some time now. You can find more of his tales with the Domino Lady, the Moon Man, and others by checking out his author's profile at Amazon, https://amazon.com/author/kevinfindley . It's also a great place to leave him a message about how much you enjoyed his first novella.

THE ROBIN HOOD OF THE PULPS

THE ROBIN HOOD OF THE 1930'S RETURNS!

Detective Sgt. Stephen Thatcher is the son of Police Chief Peter Thatcher. Sickened by the effects of the Great Depression on Great City, the young lawman cannot reconcile the rich society elite living the good life while across town the poor of Great City go hungry. Unable to correct this injustice through the system he represents, Thatcher assumes the role of the vigilante thief the Moon Man by disguising himself behind a one-way Argus glass globe. In this get up he then proceed to rob the rich and give to the needy via his loyal aide, former boxer Ned "Angel" Dargan. He is also aided by the lovely Sue McEwen, the daughter of the man sworn to capture him, his own boss, Lt. Detective Gil McEwen.

Created by pulp legend Frederick C. Davis, the Moon Man's exploits appeared in the pages of "Ten Detective Aces" and was a reader favorite. Now he returns to the streets of Great City in new thrilling adventures written by some of New Pulp's most creative writers! Pulpdom's most bizarre hero is back on the case. The enigmatic MOON MAN!

GENE MOYERS
GREG HATCHER
TERRY ALEXANDER
TIM HOLTER BRUCKNER

AN AIRSHIP 27 PRODUCTION

Pulp Fiction for a New Generation!
airship27hangar.com

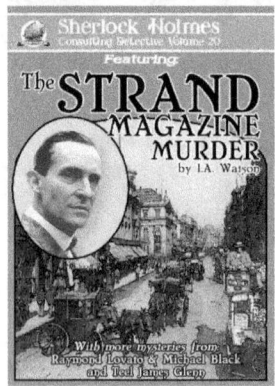
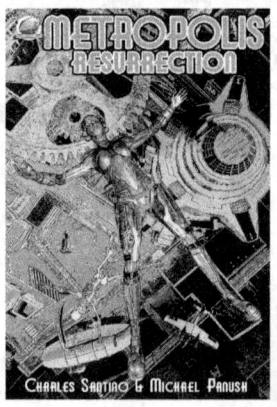

www.ingramcontent.com/pod-product-compliance
Lightning Source LLC
Chambersburg PA
CBHW051145260626
47170CB00005B/1969